Tanner and his team are done helping with cleaning up Gillham, and they're looking for something more interesting, like the string of burglaries that happened recently. What Tanner was not looking for was his mate — although he wouldn't have said no to a boyfriend — but after he meets Orlando, he's ready to make space for him in his life.

Meeting Tanner is the worst thing that could happen to Orlando. He wants to be with his mate, but Tanner is an enforcer, while Orlando is the cat shifter thief responsible for the recent burglaries. He's already decided to retire and settle down with his best friend and his mate, but first, he has one last job to do.

When Tanner finds the thief in the mayor's house, the last thing he expects is for the cat shifter to turn into Orlando. When Orlando tells him they're mates, Tanner knows he can't give him up to the authorities, so he lets him go. But Tanner is an enforcer. No matter how much he wants to be with Orlando, he doesn't know if he can ever trust him.

When there's another burglary, will Tanner be able to see through the pain of betrayal and believe Orlando has nothing to do with it? Or will they lose the fragile relationship they've managed to build?

Tanner
Copyright © 2021 Catherine Lievens
ISBN: 978-1-4874-3270-6
Cover art by Angela Waters

Published by eXtasy Books Inc or
Devine Destinies, an imprint of eXtasy Books Inc

Look for us online at:
www.eXtasybooks.com or www.devinedestinies.com

Tanner
Council Enforcers 25

By

Catherine Lievens

CHAPTER ONE

Tanner walked down the sidewalk, following his team. He could see several of them on the other side of the street, and he was pretty sure Rose had snuck into the coffee shop. Maybe she was just checking out what was happening there, or maybe she wanted coffee. Tanner wasn't going to try to keep her away from it. It wasn't his business if she stepped away from work for a moment, and no one wanted an under-caffeinated Rose. She got grumpy.

Tanner wasn't part of any of the conversations happening around him, probably because even though he was part of the team, he hadn't been for long. There had recently been an influx of new enforcers and a departure of others who had better things to do than being sent out on missions and wanted to focus on family and love, and Tanner didn't blame them. He wasn't crazy about the fact that he'd had to move to another team, but that had nothing to do with his new team.

Tanner didn't like change. He supposed he should be relieved he'd been able to stay in Gillham instead of being transferred to another town. He had Bran to thank for that, and he had.

"It's hard to look at the town and see this," someone murmured close by.

Tanner tried to understand who had spoken. He was pretty sure it was Lorcan, who'd grown up in Gillham like Tanner.

"We're fixing it," Justin answered. "And most of the people here are okay. I think that's the best we could expect, considering what happened."

1

Tanner agreed. After the Beasts had attacked Gillham, the town needed a good cleanup. Before the gang had arrived, a lot of windows had been boarded up, and it had helped. There was damage, especially close to the pack and on Main Street, but they were dealing with it. When Tanner wasn't at work patrolling the streets and making sure everyone was okay, he was out there helping with cleanup. It made for a lot of work, but he didn't mind.

He wasn't like most of his team. He didn't have anyone waiting for him at home except for his family, and while he loved them, they weren't a mate. They weren't even a boyfriend, which Tanner supposed would be easier to find. It was strange to be the only human on the team, though. Well, he wasn't, since Xander was human, too, but Xander was mated, while Tanner wasn't. Everyone on the team was either mated or in a relationship, and while Tanner was happy for them, he was also jealous.

He wanted that happiness, too. He wanted someone to go home to, talk to, and wake up with in the morning. He didn't know if he would ever find out if he was someone's mate, but even if he wasn't, he could have a boyfriend. Maybe now that his life was calming down, he'd be able to meet someone.

"What do you think?" Justin asked.

It took Tanner a moment to realize Justin was talking to him. He was only half surprised to be included in the conversation. This team was close, more like a family than coworkers, and he was the new guy. They'd welcomed him, though, and they were trying to make him feel like he was part of it.

"I apologize. I wasn't listening."

Justin smiled, thankfully not bothered. "We were talking about the string of burglaries in the wealthy area of town. I'm surprised the mayor's house hasn't been targeted yet."

Tanner had heard about the burglaries, but their team hadn't been pulled in. Until they knew whether the thief was a shifter or a human, they wouldn't be. The enforcers only took care of shifters and paranormal creatures, so it made sense. "Maybe it's the next target," he said.

"That's what I was saying," Justin agreed. "Lorcan thinks the thief won't go to the mayor's house because it would be too obvious."

"Well, we don't know how the thief thinks, but I don't see why he shouldn't try robbing the mayor's house. The mayor is the richest man in town, after all."

Kameron might be, if he didn't spread his wealth to the town and pack. Or maybe that was pack money and not Kameron's. Tanner couldn't say he fully understood how the pack worked, not because he was human, but because he hadn't asked and it wasn't his business.

"I think it would be too dangerous for him," Lorcan said.

"I think it might not be a guy," Justin added.

Tanner agreed. He wasn't sure why he'd said *he*, although something told him the thief was a guy. "What about the human police? Have they found out anything about the thief?" he asked. He was glad to be included in the conversation, and he didn't want it to end.

He and the rest of the team were patrolling the streets of Gillham. The Beasts were long gone, but that didn't mean the people in town felt safe. It helped to see the enforcers walk along the sidewalks, even though there wasn't much work to do. Tanner didn't mind, but he wished he could be out there helping clean up and rebuild instead of walking around. At least this allowed him to spend more time with his new team, which he sorely needed.

He hadn't been transferred long before they'd been thrown into the war with the Beasts. There hadn't been a lot of time to get to know the others, and Tanner would feel better once he did. They were his team, and he needed to be able to trust them to have his back at all times.

And he did. They were good people, and Bran wouldn't have put him with this team if he didn't think they would be a good fit. Tanner needed more than that, though. He needed to get to know these people as well as he knew his own family, which was what he was trying to do.

"As far as I know, they have no idea what's going on," Lorcan said. "I wouldn't be surprised if they eventually reached out to the pack to have them step in. It can't continue this way."

"I do know that they will. So far, the thief has only robbed houses in the affluent area of town. That area isn't big. How many houses are left for him to go to?"

"You think he'll eventually leave, and we'll never know what happened?"

"It's possible." But Tanner was curious.

He wanted to know who was doing this, especially to a town that was still trying to recover from being attacked by a gang. The wealthy area of Gillham hadn't been touched by the fighting, which was a surprise. Maybe the Beasts hadn't had the time to go there, or maybe they'd decided to focus on the pack since they'd been after the alpha. Tanner couldn't say he understood how the Beasts thought, and he didn't want to.

What was going on didn't sit right with him. It didn't matter that the thief kept himself to the wealthy area of town. The things he was taking weren't his, and he had no right to do it. But it wasn't Tanner's business. The team hadn't been brought in, and they might never be. Even if the police went to Kameron and Bran for help, Bran could choose another team. There were more than enough of them around.

Tanner should focus on the work he was doing and on getting to know his new team. Whatever happened next, he'd have plenty of time to deal with it later. Talking about this case wasn't bad, though, especially if it brought him, Lorcan, and Justin closer. Sometimes, it felt like the relationships between the team members were so tightly knit that Tanner had no place there.

He didn't want that to be the case.

"I think that whoever is doing this is going to try to rob the mayor," Justin declared. "Only an idiot would leave before doing that. Besides, the mayor kind of deserves it."

Tanner grimaced. "I don't think anyone deserves to be robbed."

"I would agree normally, but the mayor is an asshole. Did you know he hid in his house while the pack was attacked and that he refused to send help? Not that we needed it, but still. Anyone else would have at least offered their police officers. The pack is part of Gillham, and some pack members live here rather than in pack territory. The police should protect them, but instead, they didn't do anything."

Tanner hadn't been aware of that, but he still didn't know if it was reason enough to hope the mayor would be robbed. They were going to have to wait and see what happened, but unfortunately, Tanner had never been the most patient of men.

Orlando was curled up on the couch in his cat form when the front door slammed. He jumped, his paws slipping on the floor as he tried to hide under the couch. It took him a moment to realize he didn't have to hide, because it wasn't the police coming to arrest him but his best friend, Quincy.

"Where the fuck are you?" Quincy called out.

Orlando peeked from under the couch. He was tempted to stay where he was, but Quincy knew him better than he knew himself most of the time. He would know what Orlando was doing—hiding. There were many places in the apartment where he could hide, but there was no way out from under the couch, not unless he wanted Quincy to see him.

Quincy was pissed. Orlando wondered what he'd done to anger his best friend this time, but he wouldn't find out unless he left the couch and talked to Quincy. He didn't want to, but Quincy was one step ahead of him.

A face suddenly appeared at the edge of the couch. Orlando scrambled back, but when Quincy reached for him, he allowed his best friend to grab him without scratching him. Quincy dragged him away from the couch and raised him until they were eye to eye. Orlando made a purring sound, hoping to make his best friend smile, but Quincy was frowning.

"Why were you under the couch?" Quincy asked.

Orlando arched a brow, which wasn't easy to do as a cat. Quincy shook his head and settled Orlando on the couch, but instead of giving him privacy to shift, he stood there, his arms crossed over his chest, staring.

Orlando sighed. It wasn't like Quincy had never seen him naked anyway. He shifted, grabbed one of the pillows, and pulled it closer. Quincy snatched it away from him.

"You're not going to use this to hide your dick," he said.

"What am I supposed to use to hide it, then?"

"I don't care. And get your naked ass off my couch."

"I can shift back if it makes you feel better."

Quincy pointed a finger at Orlando's nose. "I don't think so. You and I need to talk, and we need to talk now."

Orlando swallowed. "Do you want me to go?" He expected Quincy to have enough of him eventually, but he'd hoped it would take a bit longer. He wanted to spend time with Quincy, but he understood why Quincy didn't. He had his own life, a job, friends, and more often than not, Orlando was a problem to deal with rather than a friend.

"Did I say I wanted you to go? I didn't, so get that out of your head. You're my best friend, and you can stay for as long as you need or want to. But we need to talk about what you're doing when you're not with me or at the restaurant. How many houses have you robbed since you arrived?"

"I'm not sure. Why? Does it matter?"

"Why does it matter? It matters because you shouldn't be doing it."

"I only steal from people who can afford it."

Quincy threw the pillow at Orlando's head. Orlando caught it and lowered it to his lap. He knew Quincy wasn't a hundred percent comfortable with nudity, maybe because he wasn't a shifter.

Quincy glared. "You don't know that."

"They live in big houses. They have a lot of expensive stuff. They *can* afford it," Orlando protested.

Quincy had never understood why he did what he did, and Orlando was glad for that. Quincy had grown up with his family, being loved and having everything he needed. Not that Orlando attributed the fact that he was a thief to the way he'd grown up, but that was when it had started. After aging out of the foster system, he'd had to rely only on himself, and it had been easy to use his cat form to sneak into houses and steal things he could sell to buy food.

Quincy had tried more than once to get Orlando to stop, but Orlando didn't want to rely on him too much. Quincy shouldn't have to be responsible for Orlando. They were best friends, but nothing more, and Orlando had to be able to stand on his own two feet.

But Quincy didn't like the way Orlando went about it. Orlando couldn't say he was crazy about what he did, even though every time he snuck into a house, he could feel a thrill deep in his stomach. He was doing something that could get him in trouble if he was found out, and even though so far no one had realized the thief was a shifter, he knew eventually someone would.

He'd been caught a few times. It had been easy to shift into his cat form and act like a stray cat who had snuck in. He'd had to leave everything he'd started to steal inside the house, but that didn't matter. He had more than enough money not to have to work for the rest of his life, and he had to admit that the only reason he was still stealing was a thrill it created in him. He wasn't doing it to survive anymore but to help others survive. Quincy knew that, but it still didn't make him okay with Orlando's job.

Quincy pinched the bridge of his nose and closed his eyes. "You can't know that," he repeated. "Maybe they bought the house when they had more money. Maybe they're hurting right now, and you wouldn't be aware of that. Besides, even if they're not, you're stealing their stuff. It's theirs, bought with the money they earned, not yours to put your grubby hands on."

Orlando bit his lower lip at Quincy's harsh tone. "Maybe I should go. I don't want to be found out."

Quincy put his hands on his hips and glared. "You won't be found out if you stop doing that. I already gave you a job at the restaurant. You have a place to stay here for as long as you need. What else can I do to make you step away from that life?"

Quincy wouldn't understand if Orlando explained. He was a much better person than Orlando could ever be, which was why Orlando was always surprised to see how much Quincy cared about him. When Orlando had arrived in Gillham, he hadn't had anything with him, just a backpack. Quincy had opened his home to him and given him a job, even though Orlando didn't need it. He wanted Orlando to come back on the right side of life, which Orlando was tempted to do, even if only for his best friend.

"I don't want you to get caught," Quincy continued. "And that's what's going to happen if you continue. I can't believe you robbed the chief of police."

Orlando knew better than to smile, even though he wanted

to. He bit the inside of his cheek, hoping Quincy wouldn't realize. "I'm sorry."

Quincy snorted. "We both know that's a lie. You're not sorry. You like robbing people."

"I promise I only do it to people who can truly afford it. I know these things, Quincy. You wouldn't believe how many jewels the wife of the chief of police had. No one needs that many."

"Maybe she was keeping them because she needed to sell them in case they need money. You have no way to know what's going on in people's lives, not even the chief of police."

"Come on. That might be true, but it doesn't mean I can't be sure they won't miss it. It took them two days to realize what I did! Would anyone who truly needs those jewels have taken that long to realize they were gone?"

Quincy still looked pissed, but thankfully, he wasn't yelling at Orlando anymore. "Fine. But you have to stop this." His expression changed. He wasn't angry anymore but rather worried, which was almost worse. "I don't want anything to happen to you. I don't know what I'd do if I didn't have you in my life."

"Nothing would change."

Quincy's eyes narrowed. "How can you say that? You're my best friend, the most important person in the world to me. I don't want to lose you, not even because you're an idiot. I know better than to ask you to promise you won't do it ever again, though." He paused. "Just be careful, please. And think about it. I know you don't need to steal anymore, but if you have money problems, I can help."

Orlando didn't deserve Quincy. He'd always known that, but Quincy's words just now reinforced that knowledge. He couldn't make any promises, but maybe it *was* time to start thinking about retirement.

As soon as Tanner opened the door, the shrieks started. He steeled himself, knowing he was about to be rushed. He'd gone through this many times, but it always surprised him how much force Ella and Scott had, especially when they worked together.

The thunder of small feet pounding the floor became louder. Tanner managed to close the door and leaned against it as his niece and nephew rounded the corner, running toward him. They barreled into his legs, wrapping themselves around them, and Tanner was grateful he had the door's support because he would have fallen otherwise, and them with him.

He laughed. "I take it you guys are happy to see me?" he asked.

Ella looked up at him and nodded while Scott grinned. There was something different about him, and Tanner leaned closer.

"Are you missing a tooth?" he asked.

Scott's smile widened. "I already put it under my pillow!"

Tanner carded his fingers through his nephew's soft hair. "That's great."

The sound of someone else stepping into the entrance made Tanner look up. His mother stood there, smiling softly at him and the kids. He smiled back. "Hi, Mom. How did everything go?"

"They've been angels. I could stay."

Tanner shook his head. "It's my turn babysitting. Go home to Dad. I'm sure he'll be happy to see you. Who knows what he could come up with for dinner if you don't get there in time?"

Tanner's mother shuddered. "Last time, I refused to touch whatever was in that pan. He tried eating it, but I told him I had no intention of cleaning up after him if he was sick. I don't understand why he does that. I left him food in the fridge."

"He wants to feel like he can survive without you."

"But we both know that he can't," Tanner's mom said with a chuckle.

She moved closer and kissed his cheek. "But I'm sure you have better things to do than to babysit your niece and nephew."

Ella and Scott had already unwrapped themselves from Tanner's legs. Their heads were close together as they talked, but it only took a moment for Scott to reach out and pull on his sister's hair. Tanner had no idea what was going on, but he knew that if he didn't stop this, the rest of the evening would be made up of screams and tears. He reached down, grabbed Scott's hand, and shook his head when his nephew looked up at him.

Luckily, it only lasted a few seconds. Then the kids started running one after the other, disappearing deeper inside the house, and Tanner knew he was in for a long evening. "What did you feed them? Coffee and sugar?"

His mother laughed. "It was tempting, but no. That's just how they are naturally. Your sister shouldn't be back too late, though. Just make sure they get their bath, eat dinner, and head to bed."

As far as Tanner was concerned, that was like trying to herd cats, but he'd volunteered for it, and he wouldn't back down. "Go home," he told his mother as he pushed away from the door. "I'll be fine. If I need help, I'll make sure to call Beth and Martin." But they deserved their date night, and Tanner would do everything he could to give them the chance to have fun.

He was used to dealing with Ella and Scott. He'd been in their life since they'd been born, and this wasn't the first time he babysat for his sister. It took a bit of work, but by eight PM, he had both of them fed, clean, and in bed. Scott was still chattering with his stuffed animals, but as long as he stayed in bed, Tanner wasn't going to protest. He kept an ear open just in case as he headed downstairs, but the house was quiet.

He flopped onto the couch and took a deep breath. Now he only had to wait for Beth and Martin to come back.

The team had headed to the bar after work, and to Tanner's surprise, they'd invited him to come along. They wanted to spend time getting to know him, and he wished he could have said yes. He'd already promised to babysit the kids, though, and he hadn't hidden it. He loved the kids, and he wasn't ashamed that he took care of them. Thankfully, the team hadn't seen anything wrong with that. They told him he knew where to find them if he wanted, and they headed to the bar, leaving him there wishing he could go with them. Another time, though.

Tanner opened his eyes and sat up straighter. He reached for his backpack next to the couch and took out the knitting he was working on. It was almost Ella's birthday, and he hoped to have the sweater done by then. He'd chosen a soft dark pink wool he knew she would love.

He was so focused on his work that it took him a moment to hear the door. It was only when it slammed shut and made him jump that he realized someone was home. A few seconds later, Beth called out, "Tanner?"

"In the living room." Tanner started packing his stuff. He peeked at his phone, frowning when he saw it was only nine.

Beth came into the living room. "Thanks for staying with the kids. Everything okay?" she asked. She sat on the armrest of the couch and took off one heel.

"They're both in bed, fed and clean, just like you wanted. Why are you and Martin already home?"

She shook her head. "Only me. He had to go to the hospital."

Tanner grimaced. "What happened?"

"I don't know. He's going to be late, though. I think it was a car accident."

Beth didn't berate her husband for being needed at work, even on date night. Tanner didn't know if he would feel the same way, which was why he'd never dated a doctor.

"But since I'm here, you can head out. I'm sure you have better things to do than babysit my kids," Beck continued.

"Did you talk to Mom? Because she tried to stay using the same words."

"I'm glad you didn't let her. She might have ended up with food poisoning if Dad tried cooking her dinner. And no, I didn't talk to her. I'll text her as soon as you're gone, though. What will you do?"

Tanner wondered if he should head home, but it wasn't that late. "Probably head to the bar. The team is there, and they invited me to go."

Beth slapped Tanner's shoulder. "You should have gone."

"And I am. You guys always come first, though. You know that."

"And I understand, but you have to live your own life."

Tanner got to his feet and kissed his sister's hair. "I am, and I'm happy. Stop fretting."

He texted Lorcan on his way out and got a text back almost instantly. They were still at the bar, so instead of heading to his apartment, that was where he went.

The place was crowded when he got there, and it took him a moment to find the team. They were all gathered around several tables at the back, and Tanner noticed that the mates and significant others were there, too. He was the only one missing, and he was glad he'd managed to come by.

Cedric grinned at him when he saw him. Devon was a bit more reserved, but Tanner didn't mind. He knew their back-story, and he didn't expect anything from them.

"Jonathan didn't say you were coming," Cedric said.

"That's because he didn't know. I had to babysit my sister's kids, but she came back early."

Cedric's eyes widened. "You babysit your sister's kids? That has to be adorable."

Tanner laughed. "I don't know about that, but they're pretty cute."

"I'm sure you need a beer by now. Why don't you head to the bar and grab one? We'll be here when you come back. Lorcan is already there."

Tanner slapped a few shoulders and said hello as he moved toward the bar. Everyone seemed happy to see him, which made him smile. He might not completely be part of the team for now, but he was working hard, and he knew that in no time they would feel as much his family as his old team had.

"I don't think I should be doing this," Orlando said, staring at the bar from the sidewalk.

Quinn glared at him. "Don't you want to meet my friends?"

"I'm your friend."

"My other friends, then. But I guess you don't *have* to meet them if you're going to leave."

Quincy was trying to make Orlando feel guilty—with good results. Orlando huffed. He owed a lot to his best friend, and he was ready to do pretty much anything Quincy wanted, especially after the conversation they'd had earlier. If Quincy wanted him to meet his friends, Orlando would go along with it.

"Fine. I'll meet your friends." Even though he didn't like it.

Quincy's expression softened. "You don't have to worry about their mates, I promise. I know they're enforcers, but it doesn't mean they're going to arrest you in the middle of the bar. No one but me knows what you're up to. I'm not about to tell anyone. I don't want to lose you."

"I never thought you'd tell anyone. It just makes me nervous. What if I say something I shouldn't?"

"You better watch what comes out of your mouth, I guess. Now come on. They're waiting for me."

Orlando nodded and followed Quincy inside the bar. It wasn't the first time they came there, so Orlando was comfortable with the place. What he wasn't comfortable with was the people he was about to meet.

Quincy was friends with a few guys in town. That didn't surprise Orlando, and he wasn't jealous. He'd moved around the country while Quincy had settled down in Gillham. He deserved to have friends, and they were probably better friends than Orlando could ever be. It made Orlando feel better to know that Quincy wasn't on his own when he wasn't here and that he still wouldn't be once he left. He'd agreed to stay for a bit longer because Quincy had asked, but he knew he couldn't stay forever.

Orlando wasn't one to settle down, especially not in a small town where someone could find out who he was and what he was doing.

The smell of beer and bar food hit him as soon as he walked into the place. He took a deep breath, wrinkling his nose at the sound his stomach made. He and Quincy had eaten dinner, but apparently Orlando was still hungry. He would grab some nachos along with his beer once he and Quincy settled down.

The place was loud, with so many people crowded inside, the TV on, and players arguing over a game of pool in a corner. It was cleaner than Orlando expected any bar to be, though, which was a plus in Orlando's list. What wasn't a plus was the group of people gathered at the end of the room. They'd pushed several tables together because there were so many of them, and of course, that was the group Quincy headed for as soon as he saw them.

Orlando took a deep breath and followed him. He kept an ear open to the conversations, not surprised that he heard a smaller group talk about the burglaries as soon as he was close enough. He swallowed and made sure not to look at them, instead focusing on Quincy.

"Orlando?" Quincy asked.

Orlando plastered a smile on his face. "That would be me." He turned his attention to the two guys Quincy was hovering next to and offered them his hand. "I'm Quincy's best friend, or at least, I'd like to think I am. Pleasure to meet you."

One of the guys limited himself to shaking Orlando's hand and murmured that his name was Devon, but the other arched a brow. "Since Quincy himself told us you're his best friend, you better believe it. I'm Cedric."

"Cedric and Devon. I think Quincy mentioned someone else in your little group of friends."

"That would be Yedley, but he's not here tonight, or rather, he's here, but he's helping his brother." Cedric tilted his chin toward the bar.

When Orlando turned, he saw two Nix working. To him, most Nix looked like each other, so he couldn't say whether or not these two were related, but he had no reason to doubt what Cedric had just told him.

"I should grab something to drink for both of us," Quincy said.

Orlando shook his head and pushed him toward his friends. "Stay here. I'll go, and you can talk with your friends."

"I brought you here so *you* would get to know them."

No doubt so Orlando would decide to stay in Gillham after all. It was what Quincy had been aiming at since Orlando had arrived, and while Orlando understood, he still didn't think it was a good idea. "I'll get to know them as soon as we have something to drink."

Quincy looked like he wanted to push, but thankfully, Cedric caught his attention, and Quincy let him go. Cedric winked at Orlando as he moved toward the bar, something that almost made Orlando laugh out loud.

Maybe he wouldn't mind living in Gillham after all. He doubted he ever would, if anything because of what he'd done and the fear of being found out, but it wouldn't be a problem to visit.

There was a line to get to the bar, so he stood behind the last person and waited. He kept an ear open to the conversations, but even though some people were talking about the burglaries, they had no way to know he was involved. He tried to convince himself of that and to relax, but it was hard. The last thing he wanted was to get Quincy in trouble, or of course, to be caught.

He turned when he heard two guys mentioning something about the mayor's house. He'd been thinking about sneaking inside to see if there was anything worth stealing, which he was pretty sure was the case, considering how much money the mayor made. Orlando didn't know if it was family money or if the mayor of a small town truly earned that much, but he was curious to find out if he could.

"You still think he's going to go to the mayor's house?" one of the guys asked.

He was as tall as Orlando, which Orlando enjoyed in a man. He also enjoyed the strong shoulders and the way the guy's muscles strained his t-shirt. He had short brown hair, and from the way he moved and behaved, Orlando was pretty sure he was law enforcement. That was enough for him to decide to stay away, no matter how hot the guy was. Pity, though.

"I don't see why he shouldn't. I'm pretty sure the mayor is

the wealthiest guy in town," the second guy said.

"Doesn't mean the thief is an idiot. He has to know the mayor has the best security system he could get his hands on."

"It didn't stop the thief the other times."

"But now people know he's in town. He'd be an idiot to try anything else, especially something everyone expects him to do."

Orlando hummed as he listened. Hot guy wasn't wrong—now that people were aware of his presence, they were on high alert, which would make it harder for him to find his way inside houses. It didn't mean he wasn't going to try. He liked the challenge.

The two guys walked past him, both of them holding a beer. The hot one—although the other guy wasn't bad to look at either—jostled Orlando as he passed him. His gaze snapped to Orlando, and he reached out to steady him with his free hand. "Sorry about that," he said.

Orlando could only croak. His lips were moving, but no words were coming out, which was a blessing, because he was pretty sure he would have blurted out that this guy was his mate to the guy's face.

"Tanner?" the other guy asked.

Tanner was still looking at Orlando. "You're okay?" he asked.

Orlando nodded and kept his lips pressed together. Tanner stared at him for a moment longer, then he stepped away with a smile. Orlando watched him for a few seconds, then rushed toward the door. He needed out, and he needed it *now*.

He sucked in a breath as soon as he was outside. This couldn't be his life. Here he was, a thief, and his mate was part of law enforcement. Fate truly had a twisted sense of humor. And since Tanner hadn't said anything, Orlando was pretty sure that he was either human or a paranormal being who didn't have mates. There was no other explanation.

That meant that no one would find out as long as Orlando didn't tell anyone about it.

But of course, nothing was ever that simple in his life. The bar door opened, revealing Quincy. Orlando resisted the urge to run away, knowing his best friend would get his hands on him either way.

"What's going on?" Quincy asked. "Already running?"

Orlando shook his head. He didn't want to tell Quincy because he suspected Quincy would be delighted to find out about this. He wanted Orlando to move to Gillham, and having his mate there was one more reason to do it. Orlando wasn't sure, but he also knew he couldn't keep it to himself.

"Something happened," he whispered.

His tone was enough to tell Quincy that whatever was happening was serious. He moved closer, gently touching Orlando's shoulder. "What is it?"

"One of the guys at the bar. He's my mate."

Quincy sucked in a breath. "Who?"

Orlando shook his head. "Does it matter? I don't know what to do."

Quincy's hand tightened. "The way I see it, you have a choice to make. Either you leave, or you stay and stop stealing."

And Orlando knew exactly which option Quincy wanted him to choose. What he didn't know was whether he could do it.

Chapter Two

For some reason, Tanner couldn't stop thinking about the guy from the bar. Nothing had happened beyond him knocking into the guy as he walked by, but he couldn't shake the feeling that somehow, something had. He hadn't failed to notice how quickly the guy had left the bar after that, which made him wonder what had happened.

He wasn't quite sure how to find out. He didn't want to ask around, but he suspected that was the only way for him to find out who the guy was. He'd noticed that someone from their group had gone after him, but he didn't know that guy, either. It would be fairly easy to find out through Cedric and Devon, though. They'd been talking to the second guy, so they had to know who he was. Hopefully, it meant their mates knew, too.

Right now, the team was relaxing in the enforcers' house after a day of work. They were skipping the bar today, which was more than okay with Tanner. He enjoyed getting a beer with his friends, but he could do without the crowd and with an evening home, since it was still fairly early. This place was just as crowded, but at least it felt more like he was home rather than in a public place. Here, he could take his boots off and even work on his knitting, something he wouldn't have dared doing at the bar or even the coffee shop. He didn't care what people thought about him knitting, but he could do without the whispers and outright scorn.

The enforcers didn't care, at least most of them, and those who did knew better than to confront him about it. He needed to finish the sweater for Ella, which was why he was knitting as he listened to his friends talking. He was waiting for the right moment to ask Lorcan and Jonathan about their mates and their friend, but so far, he hadn't had any luck. He was going to have to make his own.

He waited for a laugh and a break in the conversation, and when it happened, he waved at Jonathan. "There's something I want to ask you."

Jonathan's eyebrows rose, but he leaned closer. "What is it?"

"Last night, I noticed someone was talking to your mate and Devon. Do you happen to know who it is?"

Jonathan looked even more surprised, while Lorcan, who was sitting on his other side, grinned. "Are you interested in Quincy?"

"Not in him."

"Oh, so you *are* interested in someone."

Tanner realized it was a trap, but he couldn't blame Lorcan for it. He knew his teammates were curious about him, and he wasn't usually one to talk about his private life. "I wouldn't say interested. But I bumped into Quincy's friend on my way from the bar, and he kind of freaked out. I'm pretty sure he left, which made me curious and worried. I hope I didn't do anything to offend or hurt him." Tanner couldn't think of anything, but what did he know?

Jonathan frowned. "Cedric did mention something about Quincy's best friend being there, but he said the guy left before they could get to know him. He wasn't happy about it, and he sounded a bit worried. It makes more sense now, after what you said."

"But Tanner wouldn't have done anything to hurt this guy," Lorcan said.

The confidence in him touched Tanner. "I didn't. The only thing I can think of is that I bumped into him, but I apologized, and he seemed okay." He'd also seemed stunned, which didn't make sense. Tanner was sure they'd never met before last night. Something more was going on, or maybe he was just obsessing over nothing. At this point, he didn't know anymore.

"I'm sure we can find out his name through Cedric," Jonathan said. "Let me text him."

"You don't have to do it now. It can wait." Tanner had been looking forward to an evening at home, although he couldn't deny that trying to find the guy was more appealing.

"It's not a problem. Besides, I'm sure Cedric will be happy to help."

Tanner thought Jonathan was right, but he wasn't looking forward to Cedric sticking his nose into this situation. As much as he loved the guy, he didn't love his nosiness. He wouldn't say anything about it, not after what Cedric had gone through, but it was always better when he was focused on someone else.

Jonathan was already texting, though, so Tanner did his best to relax. He tried to focus on his knitting and listening to the conversations around him, but every time he did, the guy's face appeared in his mind.

What was it with him that fascinated Tanner so much?

The guy was hot. Maybe that was why Tanner couldn't stop thinking about him. He was tall but thin, with long blond hair and brown eyes. The bar had been fairly dark, but even in the darkness, Tanner had been able to see the freckles on the guy's nose. There weren't very many, just enough for him to be able to count them if they ever were in a more private situation.

Then there was the nose ring. Tanner had never been into pierced guys, but that delicate hoop around the guy's nostril fit him perfectly and made Tanner want to check whether he had other piercings.

"His name is Orlando," Jonathan said suddenly.

Tanner knew he wouldn't be knitting anymore tonight, so he put away his things as Jonathan and Lorcan talked. Once he felt a bit steadier, he faced Jonathan. "What did Cedric say?"

"Not a lot. Like I said, Orlando is Quincy's best friend. Quincy is Cedric's friend, not Orlando, so Cedric doesn't know much about him. He said Quincy has a restaurant in town and that Orlando works for him for now. Cedric got the impression that Orlando isn't going to stick around for long, or at least that he's not used to sticking around. He offered to talk to Quincy, although considering the hour, Quincy's at work."

Tanner tapped his fingertips on his thigh. "Which restaurant?" This decision would probably come back to bite him in the ass, but he wanted to see Orlando again. What better way to do that than to get some dinner?

Jonathan smiled. "I like the way you think. I'll text you the name and address. Are you going there on your own?"

He could, although he could easily imagine how stupid he would look eating dinner on his own, especially if it was a nice restaurant. "I'll probably take my sister."

Martin was at home tonight, and he wouldn't be available even for emergencies. It was his night off, and while Tanner was sure that Beth wanted to spend time with her husband, he also knew she would enjoy time away from her kids. Tanner knew from experience how much of a handful they could be. As long as they had dinner early, she would probably be up for going out.

"Introducing your sister to the guy you like before you even talk to him? That's brave," Lorcan commented.

"He's not a guy I like. I just want to make sure he's okay."

"And why do you think that is?"

"I feel responsible. He freaked out after I bumped into

him."

Jonathan nodded, but Lorcan didn't look convinced. "Whatever you say, I know there's something more there."

"I don't know what to tell you." Tanner got to his feet. If he was going to go home to change and pick up Beth, he needed to get moving. "But I'll let you know how tonight goes. Don't get your hopes up. I just want to check on the guy and apologize if I did something I shouldn't have."

"I don't think you can blame yourself if the only thing you did was bump into him. Hopefully, you don't freak him out even more by popping up at his place of work and trying to talk to him."

Tanner frowned. He hadn't thought about that, but he should have. He wanted to apologize for freaking Orlando out, but what if appearing at the restaurant made Orlando freak out even more?

He wouldn't find out until he did this, and he couldn't think of a better way to do it. He might get an address through Cedric, but that would be even worse. A phone number could be enough, but for some reason, he needed to see Orlando's face, and Tanner had learned a long time ago to follow his instincts. They were telling him that trying to talk to Orlando was the right thing to do, so that was what he would try first.

Orlando wasn't sure he would ever get used to being a waiter. He'd thought it would be an easy job, and he wanted to help Quincy. Doing this was anything but easy, though.

He loathed dealing with customers. Most of them were okay people, but a few were pains in the ass, and not in the way he liked it. He wanted to tell them to fuck off, but he didn't want Quincy to have problems, especially after opening his home to him and giving him a job. So he gritted his teeth and smiled, even at people who didn't deserve a smile, and he continued working. It didn't matter that his feet ached and that he wanted nothing more than to run away.

He owed it to Quincy.

Orlando didn't need to work. The only reason he was doing this was that it helped Quincy, but also because Quincy didn't like thinking about how Orlando used the money he'd stolen to survive. Orlando didn't understand it, but then he supposed Quincy didn't understand how he could steal for a living.

Orlando stumbled into the kitchen with his arms full of dirty plates. He set them down next to the sink, and when he turned, he wasn't surprised to see Quincy staring at him.

Quincy was a bit sweaty, and his cheeks were flushed. He was at home here in the kitchen, though, and he moved in a way that reminded Orlando of when he was on one of his jobs. He knew better than to say that out loud. Instead, he grumbled, "Remind me why I agreed to work for you?"

Quincy chuckled. "I don't think I allowed you to say no."

"Right." He hadn't. Once he'd realized Orlando would be here for a while, he'd decided to put him to work. Orlando hadn't been able to say no, which he was sure Quincy had been counting on. He was sneaky that way.

Quincy put down the spoon he'd been using to stir whatever was in his pan and leaned his hip against the counter. "I know you don't need to work here, and I'm grateful for the help."

"You could hire someone else to do this, maybe someone who actually needs the money."

"I could, and I probably should. Who would keep you out of trouble, though?"

"You're not the one keeping me out of trouble."

Quincy arched a brow. "Are you sure about that? Because as far as I'm concerned, as long as you're here working for me, you're not out there sneaking into houses." He lowered his voice. "It helps me to know that you're not doing something stupid. I realize this isn't the best arrangement, at least for you, but it gives me peace of mind."

Orlando sucked in a breath. He would do pretty much anything for Quincy, and he hated that Quincy felt that way about him. "You don't have to keep an eye on me. I'm an adult."

Quincy shook his head. "I'm aware of that. I also know that what you do for a living is dangerous, and I don't want to lose you."

It wasn't just that Quincy disapproved of what Orlando did, but also that he was afraid that Orlando would be found out and arrested. It was a fear that never left Orlando, so he could understand. "You'd be fine even if I had to go."

Quincy glared. "I know. It doesn't mean I *want* you to go." He paused. "Now, why don't you go and take the food to the customers. I'm sure people out there are hungry."

The conversation was over, at least for now. That was probably a good thing. The restaurant's kitchen wasn't the best place to talk about this with the many ears around.

Orlando snatched a few plates, checked what table they were headed out to, and went back to the restaurant's main room. He delivered the food, smiled and nodded, then turned around and froze.

Tanner was sitting at one of Orlando's tables.

He was with a woman, and they were talking. From the way they leaned toward each other, they looked close, and Orlando's stomach churned uneasily. Tanner was his mate, but he didn't know that. Could he have a girlfriend?

Orlando couldn't face him, so he rushed back to the kitchen, wondering how he was supposed to face his mate.

"What are you doing?" Quincy asked.

Orlando jumped. He'd been so focused on avoiding Tanner that he hadn't thought that Quincy wouldn't allow him to hide in the kitchen. "I need to go home."

"Why? What happened?"

"Tanner is out there."

Quincy blinked. "You mean *your* Tanner?"

Orlando glared. "He's not my anything. But yes, he's sitting there, and he's with a woman."

"And that stops you from serving them, why?"

"You *know* why."

"Look, Orlando. I understand why you're freaking out, but I think we should just ignore Tanner. You haven't decided what you're going to do, and if you're going to leave, you probably shouldn't talk to him."

"Don't you think it would be his right to know we're mates?"

"I don't know. I can only talk about myself, but if my mate was planning on leaving me behind, I don't think I'd want to know. It's easy for humans to live without their mate, especially if they don't even know they've met them. I think that until you make a decision, you should stay away from him. Ask one of the other waiters to take care of the table."

Orlando nodded and peeked out into the main room again. What Quincy was saying made sense, but Orlando had so many questions. Who was that woman? Was she Tanner's girlfriend? So far, they'd only talked, and Orlando hadn't seen them kiss or anything like that. That didn't mean they weren't together, though.

He wanted to know. He probably had no right, since he still wasn't sure whether he should tell Tanner they were mates, but he couldn't help but wonder. Besides, what if he decided to stay? What if he tried telling Tanner they were mates and Tanner told him that he already had someone in his life and that they couldn't be together? Then Orlando would regret staying, and he didn't want that to happen. He also didn't want to walk around Gillham knowing his mate was out there and possibly seeing him, while also knowing Tanner would never be his.

No matter how little Orlando liked it, Tanner was a huge part of his life. Orlando couldn't decide whether to stay or not without taking him into account. To do that, he had to know everything he could about Tanner, or at the very least, whether Tanner was with someone.

"Are you still trying to hide?" Quincy asked.

"I'm not hiding."

"You are." Quincy sighed. "Look, if you can't deal with this, you should go home. I won't blame you for that. I might be human, but I can imagine what it feels like to meet your mate. If you don't want to talk to Tanner, that's fine. I doubt he's here to see you anyway."

That hurt more than it should have, but it was true. Tanner was only here to have dinner with his friend—maybe girl-friend—because how could he have known that Orlando worked here? Why would he have wanted to know? Orlando was nothing to him, and he probably didn't even remember him.

This had to be a coincidence, and it wasn't a happy one, as far as Orlando was concerned. The problem was that he couldn't stay away—and that he didn't *want* to. If this was his only chance to be close to Tanner, he was going to take it.

He straightened. "I'm not going home," he declared.

Quincy looked amused. "Good. That means you have work to do, and you should start. Remember that here, I'm your boss. I can fire you anytime I want."

Orlando grinned. "You wouldn't. You love me too much."

"And sometimes, I don't remember why. Now shoo."

Orlando sucked in a breath and went.

Beth looked around, obviously pleased. "I don't think I've

ever been here. It looks nice, and I've heard good things about the place."

Tanner smiled. He was pretty sure his sister knew he was distracted, but so far, she hadn't asked why. She would eventually, and he didn't know how he would answer, but he didn't think it mattered. She was his sister and one of his best friends.

"I wasn't expecting your invitation to go out for dinner," Beth continued.

"I thought you could do with a night away from the two hellions you call children."

She laughed. "I can't say I was sorry to leave them in Martin's hands. I love them to bits, but god, you don't know how exhausted I am by the end of the day."

Tanner had babysat them so much that he could easily imagine, which was one of the reasons he was happy to do this for Beth. She'd warned him she needed to be home early, but that wouldn't be a problem.

A door at the back of the room opened, and Tanner saw a glimpse of the kitchen through it. That was all he noticed, though, because Orlando walked through the door, his back straight, an obviously fake smile pasted on his face. He made a beeline for Tanner and Beth's table, and Tanner readied himself, although he wasn't sure for what.

"Good evening, and welcome," Orlando said. His voice was smooth and practiced. "Can I bring you something to drink to start?"

Tanner beamed at him. "You can. A soda is fine for me, and what about you, Beth?" he asked, turning to his sister.

She was looking at him as if he'd lost his mind. "The same."

Orlando nodded and took a note in his notepad. "I'll go grab that and the menus for you."

Tanner couldn't let him leave without asking his question. That was why he was here in the first place. "Are you okay?"

Orlando blinked and stared at him. "Why wouldn't I be?"

"I don't know. You ran away when we bumped into each other last night."

Orlando's cheeks reddened. The ring in his nostril glinted under the warm lights, which made Tanner want to look at it closer, maybe even close enough to be able to kiss Orlando. Would he let Tanner kiss him? That was what Tanner was here to find out, at least in part.

"I'm fine," Orlando said.

Tanner might have believed him if he hadn't dropped his pen just then. He reached for it at the same time Tanner did, and their fingers brushed. Orlando jerked back, dropping his notepad next.

Tanner pressed his lips together so he wouldn't smile. Whatever had happened, Orlando was flustered about his presence here, which boded well. He hadn't thought about more than making sure Orlando was okay when he decided to do this, but maybe there was more to it. His presence flustered Orlando, it had when they'd met at the bar, too. For some reason, Tanner wanted to find out more about him and was fascinated. All of that pointed at something between them, although what that something was, Tanner wasn't sure.

"Sorry about that," Orlando said as he straightened. "I'll be right back."

He turned around and left, apparently as quickly as he could and without looking where he was going, because he hit his hip on the corner of the table next to Tanner and Beth's. Luckily, no one was eating there, and Orlando quickly straightened it before leaving.

Tanner watched him go. Orlando was thin, and there seemed to be little muscle on him—Tanner would be more than happy to find out what was hiding under his clothes—but his butt looked like it had been made in heaven specifically for Tanner.

"Okay, what's going on?" Beth asked suddenly. She sounded like the question had burst out of her. She was staring at Tanner like he'd grown a second head.

"To be honest, I'm not sure yet."

"Why did you want to come to this place? Is it because of the waiter?"

Tanner looked around, but no one was paying attention to them. He should have known better than to think he could hide a secret from Beth, especially when he no doubt was obvious about it. "His name is Orlando. I met him last night, although we didn't have the opportunity to talk. He's friends with some of the mates from my team."

"That doesn't explain why you decided to eat here."

"I *might* be interested. But I'm not sure there can be anything between us," he added in a rush before his sister could make too much of it. He should have known better. She *would* make too much of this, whatever he said.

She beamed at him. "You like him."

"I'm not sure about that yet. I just wanted to make sure he was okay, because yesterday I bumped into him and sent him running out the door. That's all there is to this for now."

"But you like him. You wouldn't be worrying about him if you didn't."

Tanner had wondered why he was so fascinated by Orlando. Since they'd barely talked, it had to be because of the way Orlando looked. Tanner wasn't usually one to fixate on people's appearance, though, which made him think that maybe there was more to it, even though he couldn't understand what that *more* was. "I'm attracted to him, and I feel drawn to him. That's all I know for sure."

Beth was still smiling. "Maybe he's your mate."

Tanner blinked. "Why do you think that?"

"Well, you said you didn't even talk, yet here you are, making sure he's okay. Why would you do that if there wasn't something between you?"

"Maybe because I'm a considerate person, and I wanted to make sure I didn't hurt him?"

"You *are* a considerate person, but I think there's more to it. I've never seen you like this with anyone, not even with people you'd actually talked to and liked."

Tanner leaned back in his chair and frowned. What Beth was saying made sense, but he suspected it was wishful thinking. Wouldn't Orlando have mentioned something if he and Tanner were mates? Tanner wouldn't know, since he was human, and he had no way to know whether Orlando was, too. What if he was a shifter, though? He would no doubt have mentioned something if Tanner was his mate, especially since they'd bumped into each other.

The kitchen door opened and Orlando walked through, holding a tray with two sodas. He looked cautious as he walked toward Tanner and Beth's table, but he was smiling, although that could be because it was part of his job description.

"Here are your drinks," he said as he set the glasses onto the table. "And the menus."

Tanner took the offered menu, but he didn't open it. He couldn't stop staring at Orlando and wondering if Beth was right. Was Orlando a shifter? Was Tanner his mate?

"I'll give you a moment to go over them," Orlando continued.

Tanner was pretty sure Orlando was looking at him more than he should at any customer. Tanner couldn't stop staring, and he knew Orlando couldn't, either. Even as he moved around the room checking in with the other customers, he was always aware of where Tanner was.

"There's *definitely* something there," Beth breathed out.

Her grin told Tanner she was planning something, so he wasn't surprised when she reached out and squeezed his hand over the table. At the same moment, Orlando seemed to trip on air and almost fell on his face.

Beth cackled and withdrew her hand. "I knew it."

"You're way too amused by this." Although Tanner was, too. He hadn't expected this to happen, but he was pleased with the way Orlando reacted to his presence. Even if the mate thing *was* only wishful thinking, it didn't mean there couldn't be anything between them.

"He's coming back. Act like you're happy to see him."

"I just talked to him a few minutes ago." But Tanner *was* happy that Orlando was once again close to him, and when Orlando reached their table, he smiled.

Orlando hoped the smile plastered on his face didn't look too much like a grimace as he reached Tanner's table. He needed to know what was going on, and the best way to do that was to ask while also not asking. "Have you and your wife decided what you want to eat?" he asked.

He'd thought the woman might be Tanner's girlfriend, but he'd noticed the ring on her finger. Tanner wasn't wearing one, which gave Orlando hope, but since Tanner was an enforcer, he might not be wearing his wedding ring because it would be uncomfortable at work.

Not knowing was driving Orlando crazy, which was why he'd worded his question the way he had. That didn't mean Tanner would explain who the woman was, but Orlando hoped he would.

The woman laughed. "I'm not his wife," she explained. "I'm his sister, Beth. It's a pleasure to meet you."

Orlando's knees felt weak with his relief. "Orlando."

Beth nodded. "And in case you're wondering, Tanner is single and very much gay."

Orlando's cheeks felt like they were on fire, while Tanner

looked like he was considering hiding under the table. Maybe they could hide together. "That's . . . interesting," Orlando said. He wanted to know more, but he was working, and he didn't want Quincy to kick his ass. "Have you decided what you want to eat?"

Beth took the menu and opened it. "I'll have the lasagna."

"Chicken Alfredo for me," Tanner said. "With a salad on the side."

Orlando wrote that down, then took back the menus. "Do you want breadsticks in the meantime?"

"We're fine to wait."

Orlando was surprised to see that Tanner didn't seem to mind that his sister had outed him in the middle of a restaurant to someone they barely knew. He wanted to ask why not, but he realized he had no idea how sibling relationships worked. Even when he'd had five or six of them with him in foster care, they hadn't truly been siblings.

"Unless there's something else you can offer?" Tanner asked.

Orlando blinked, trying to understand what he was saying. With the way Tanner was looking at him, Orlando wanted to offer himself, but he doubted Beth and the other customers would be happy to see that. "Bread?" he asked. "Or you could order a starter to share."

"What would you choose if you were on a date?"

"You're not on a date," Orlando said stupidly.

"I sure hope I'm not, since I'm here with my sister. But you work here. You know what's good and what isn't."

"Everything is good. My best friend is the cook and the owner. He wouldn't allow anything not to taste good."

"I see. Why don't you surprise us, then?"

"Any allergies I need to know about?"

"We both eat just about everything."

"All right. I'll be right back."

34

It took everything he had not to run back to the kitchen, yet at the same time, he wanted to stick around and continue talking to Tanner. He'd never felt this way before, and he knew it was because Tanner was his mate, but he was starting to dislike it. Why did he have to feel so drawn to Tanner? Tanner was the worst person to be Orlando's mate. He was an enforcer, and Orlando was a cat thief. If anyone ever realized the thief was a shifter, they would pull the enforcers in, and Tanner might be on that team. He'd have to hunt and arrest Orlando, which would put a damper on their relationship, to say the least.

But they didn't have a relationship. So far, the only thing they had was awkward flirting with Tanner's sister present. Nothing else might come out of it. Orlando shouldn't *want* anything else to come out of it, but he couldn't ignore the fact that Tanner was his mate. He'd only ever have *one* of those, and while he hadn't spent most of his life dreaming about meeting his mate like a lot of shifters did, he also couldn't just ignore the bond between him and Tanner.

"Why are you in here with the menus?" Quincy asked.

Orlando blinked at him, then looked down at his hands. "What?"

Quincy looked halfway between exasperated and amused. He gestured at the menus Orlando was holding. "The menus. They don't belong in the kitchen. What's going on out there that you're so flustered?"

Orlando put the menus down onto the counter and leaned closer. "It's Tanner."

"What did he do?"

"Apart from being gorgeous? Nothing. He's here with his sister, which is sweet."

"Sweet?"

"You know what I mean."

"I know you're fascinated by good relationships between

siblings. Having dinner with your sister is nothing extraordinary for most people, though."

Orlando huffed. "Well, he's sweet with her, and she told me he's gay and single."

"Does that mean you decided to stick around and try to make things work with him?"

"No." But it made Orlando feel better. The fact that he had a chance with Tanner made him want to stay, but could he?

Quincy sighed. "I see. Well, since he's part of whatever you have going on, you should give him your number."

"How am I supposed to do that?"

"I don't know. You want me to write it in mayo on his plate?"

Orlando snorted at the thought. "I don't think that will be necessary."

"Find a way. He's not just a guy, Orlando. He's your mate. You really want to lose him without even trying?"

"I don't know what I want," Orlando murmured.

"Well, you better start thinking about it. It sounds like Tanner is interested in you, which makes sense, but how long will it continue if you don't give him anything? He doesn't know you're mates. He's not going to wait for you forever."

Quincy was right, but Orlando wasn't sure it was enough for him to make his move. He didn't want to start anything with Tanner, then decide that he needed to leave after all. And what about Tanner being an enforcer? What if he ever found out what Orlando was involved in? He would be angry, and he would be right to be.

The way Orlando saw it, he was going to have to make several decisions. He needed to decide if he wanted to stay in Gillham or leave, and if he wanted to continue stealing for a living or if it was time to retire. Orlando didn't know how to do anything else, though, and the thought of trying terrified him.

A hand on his shoulder made him jerk away, but it was only Quincy. He was frowning at Orlando, and Orlando tried to reassure him by smiling. It didn't look like it worked.

"I know you're worried," Quincy said. "I am, too. I've always wanted you to stop doing what you do and settle down close by so we could spend more time together, but I realize it might not be your dream. Your job doesn't define you, though. Even if you stop doing it, you won't stop being Orlando, and I won't stop loving you."

Orlando snorted. "If anything, you'll love me more if I stop doing it."

"I can't say I understand why you do it or that I'm happy about it. That doesn't change how I feel about you, though. You're my best friend, and you'll always be my best friend, no matter what you decide to do with your life. I'm just terrified of losing you. I can't stop thinking about what's going to happen if someone finds you and arrests you. I don't want to have to visit you in jail."

Orlando swallowed. "I'll think about it. And like you said, I have one more reason to decide to stick around now."

"I'm scared it won't be enough."

Orlando was, too. He was scared Tanner wouldn't be enough, and even more that *he* wouldn't be enough for Tanner. Tanner looked like a great guy, and Orlando suspected he deserved better than someone who stole for a living. He could stop doing it, but that wouldn't change the fact that he was a thief.

That was why he didn't write his number down for Tanner to take when he and Beth left. Tanner looked disappointed, but he didn't ask, which maybe pointed to the fact that he wasn't as interested as Orlando thought he was. Orlando didn't know, and it didn't look like he would find out any time soon.

But Gillham was a small town where everyone knew

everyone. If he wanted to find Tanner, it would be easy for him.

He just had to decide whether or not he wanted to first.

CHAPTER THREE

Tanner had to find another way to get to Orlando. He wanted to see him again, but he doubted that going to the restaurant a second time would work. He didn't want to freak him out—he'd already seemed flustered enough the other day at dinner. Tanner had hoped Orlando would give him his phone number, but he hadn't, so now Tanner had to find a way around that.

Unfortunately, the only way he could think of was to talk to Cedric and Devon and hope they wouldn't tease him too much. It would be easier if he waited until he could get them on their own, but today they were both at the enforcers' house, and Tanner wasn't willing to miss this opportunity. Besides, he also wanted to talk to Orlando as soon as possible. He knew Orlando didn't usually live in town, and he didn't want to risk Orlando leaving without finding out if there was something between them.

He located Cedric and Devon in the kitchen, along with Yedley and a few team members. Everyone nodded and smiled at him when they saw him, but he focused on the mates. He was nervous, which didn't make sense. It wasn't like he was asking for something they couldn't give him. He didn't want Orlando's phone number, although he'd be happy to get it. He just wanted a way to talk to Orlando.

Cedric grinned at him. "Are you here because you're hungry?"

Tanner couldn't help but smile back. The mates had welcomed him in the same way the team had, and that made

Tanner feel like he had a second family. "No, although I'm sure that whatever you're cooking will be delicious."

"What do you need, then? Something to drink?"

Thankfully, Tanner trusted the people in the kitchen. That didn't mean he was looking forward to explaining what he wanted in front of them. "I wanted to talk to you."

Cedric's smile widened. "Finally. I was wondering when you were going to come. For a while, I thought you'd gotten Orlando's phone number, but Quincy told me you didn't."

Tanner wasn't surprised Cedric knew about this. "I didn't ask, and he didn't offer."

"What do you want from me, then? Because I'm not sure I'm comfortable giving you his phone number if he didn't. Besides, I don't have his number. I'd have to ask Quincy."

"If I'm honest, I'm not sure. I'd just like an opportunity to talk to Orlando soon."

Cedric leaned back against the counter. "You're interested in him."

It was useless trying to hide it. "Maybe? I'd like to get to know him, that's for sure." But Tanner wasn't a hundred percent sure about what he felt. Maybe it was just curiosity. Maybe it was more. There was only one way to find out, and that was talking to Orlando.

"And you don't want to go to the restaurant again."

"I'm curious about how you found out about the restaurant, but I'm afraid to ask."

That made Cedric laugh. "I know everything there is to know in town. Also, Quincy is my friend, and he told me about it."

"He works in the kitchen, right?"

"He owns the restaurant, and he's Orlando's best friend. If there's someone who knows about Orlando, it's him." Cedric's eyes widened. "We should use him."

Tanner felt like he wasn't going to like whatever came next.

"What do you mean?"

"We need to get you and Orlando together. Since I don't want to be too involved, the best way to do that would be to coordinate with Quincy. Maybe we could get the two of you in the same places *casually*," he added, wiggling his eyebrows.

"You mean you'd have Quincy call you when Orlando is on the move and you'd drag me to wherever he's going?"

"Exactly!"

That sounded like something Tanner could go along with, but only if Orlando was okay seeing him. Hopefully, Quincy would keep that in mind. Since he was Orlando's best friend, surely he would want to keep Orlando safe, even from Tanner — or maybe especially from him. Tanner couldn't deny he felt a bit like a creep, but he didn't know how else to deal with the situation. And if Orlando told him he didn't want anything to do with him, he would disappear.

Still, aside from directly asking Orlando out, he didn't know what else to do. This was the best idea he'd heard, so he nodded. "All right. We can do that."

Cedric looked like Tanner had just handed him the moon. "Great. I happen to know that Orlando is at the coffee shop right now. We should head out."

Tanner spluttered. "This soon?"

"Why not? You want to talk to Orlando, and I know where he is. Why would you want to wait?"

Tanner didn't want to, but he'd hoped he would have a bit more time to wrap his mind around the idea and find something to say to Orlando. Instead, Cedric was already drying his hands on a towel and grabbing Tanner's wrist to drag him toward the door.

Tanner could have easily resisted, but instead, he went along with the flow. He didn't miss how amused Jonathan and the other enforcers in the kitchen were, and he rolled his eyes at them as he finally followed Cedric out of the kitchen.

Devon was trailing behind them, which surprised Tanner, but he was smiling. He didn't smile enough, as far Tanner was concerned.

"What will you tell him?" Cedric asked as they left the house.

Thankfully, Tanner's car was parked in front of it, and he guided the other two toward it. "I don't know. Do we have to act like my presence there is a coincidence?"

"Well, it would be better. We want to do this several times until Orlando falls for you, right?"

Tanner shook his head. "You have too much faith in me. I'm not even sure what I want from him."

"You might not think you know what you want, but come on. It's obvious. You like him, and you want in his pants."

Tanner unlocked the door and guided Cedric toward the passenger seat. He didn't look like he would stop talking, not even when Tanner closed the door behind him and walked around the car. Devon had settled in the back, and he smiled gently at Tanner when their gazes crossed.

Tanner slipped into the driver's seat, and Cedric was still talking. " — but if it's not just sex, it would be great."

"What are you talking about?" Tanner asked. He put his seatbelt on and turned on the engine.

"That you're the only team member who's still single. Everyone wants to see you happy with someone, and I think Orlando could be that someone."

"Or maybe he's not, and I'm just going to bother him."

"Don't talk that way. You have to have faith in yourself."

"It doesn't have anything to do with faith. I just understand that maybe I'm not Orlando's type. Maybe he won't like that I went to the restaurant and he won't want to talk to me." Tanner was ready to face just about anything, although he hoped he wouldn't have to.

He was grateful for Cedric's chatter as he drove out of pack territory and toward town. It helped him not obsess over what was going to happen. From the way Orlando had reacted to his presence at the restaurant the other night, he probably wouldn't be angry to see him, but what did he know?

He supposed he was about to find out. He couldn't remember the last time he'd been so nervous, especially when it came to guys. Whatever it was, there *was* something special about Orlando, and Tanner was going to find out what it was.

He couldn't stop wondering about what his sister had said. Could it be that he and Orlando were mates? He didn't know if Orlando was human or shifter, but he still couldn't shake off the thought that if Orlando was a shifter and they were mates, he would have said something. Why wouldn't he have?

The only reason Tanner could think of was that Orlando didn't want Tanner as a mate. The thought made his stomach churn, but he had to face it. Maybe nothing would come out of this. It wouldn't be the first time, and it certainly wouldn't be the last. Tanner had dealt with rejection before, but somehow, thinking about Orlando rejecting him felt worse than all the other times put together.

As he drove down Main Street, he knew he was about to find out what would come next for him and Orlando, and he had no idea which way things would go.

Orlando was sipping on his coffee when he noticed Cedric, Devon, and Tanner walk in front of the coffee shop. He wasn't surprised when they opened the door and walked in, but he also wasn't amused.

He turned to glare at Quincy, who was acting like he was entirely innocent. "What's going on?" he asked.

"I have no idea what you're talking about. We're having

coffee."

"Why is Tanner here?"

"Maybe he wants coffee?"

Orlando groaned. "What did you and the others do?"

Quincy leaned closer, but he kept an eye on the small group, just like Orlando. "We didn't do anything. Cedric texted and asked where I was and if you were with me. I told him we were getting coffee, and he said he and Devon would come by. I didn't know Tanner would, too."

Orlando stared at his best friend, trying to figure out if he was lying. He wasn't entirely sure, but he wouldn't put it past Quincy to have organized this. He'd been mentioning Tanner often since Tanner had come to the restaurant, and Orlando wasn't an idiot. Quincy hoped that if Orlando started dating Tanner, it would give him one more reason to stick around in Gillham.

He wouldn't be wrong. If Orlando and Tanner ever ended up together, Orlando knew he wouldn't be going anywhere. That was why he hadn't talked to Tanner yet. He wasn't sure what he wanted or what he had to offer, and this wasn't just any guy. It was his mate, and he wanted to treat Tanner with respect and avoid hurting him as much as possible.

Cedric didn't even act surprised to see Orlando and Quincy. Once he and the other two had their coffee in hand, he dragged Tanner closer, with Devon trailing behind him. "Hey," he said.

He started to sit down, but Quincy shot to his feet. "I have to talk to you and Devon."

Cedric's eyes widened comically, and he nodded. "Of course. I saw some tables outside, or we could cross the street to the park."

"I think that would be best. We should have privacy to talk about this."

Orlando glared. He was pretty sure Quincy had nothing to

talk about to Cedric and Devon and that the three of them would be peeking in through the windows to watch him and Tanner. He couldn't say it out loud, though. He didn't want to embarrass his friend, but more importantly, Tanner.

"We'll be right back," Quincy promised Orlando. "But you won't be alone, so don't worry too much, okay?"

"I won't be alone, huh?" Orlando asked.

"Tanner will keep you company until we're back."

"Shouldn't you be asking him if he can before declaring it?"

Quincy shrugged and grabbed Cedric's hand, pulling him toward the door. "See you soon."

Orlando huffed as he leaned back in his chair, but he didn't try to stop Quincy. He wouldn't be able to.

Tanner slid into the chair Quincy had just vacated, but he didn't say anything. He looked amused, though, which Orlando took as a good sign.

Orlando cleared his throat and took a sip of coffee. "They're playing matchmaker," he said.

"I think everyone can see that." Tanner sounded amused.

Orlando relaxed. Tanner wasn't angry, which was all that mattered. "Did you know about it?"

"They might have told me you and Quincy were here when they asked me out for coffee."

"Yet you said yes."

Tanner took a sip of his coffee and stared at Orlando. "Maybe because I wanted to see you."

Orlando's chest felt tight suddenly. "Now why would you want that?" he murmured.

Tanner straightened. "This was Cedric's idea, but I went along with it because I didn't know how else to get to you."

"You didn't seem to have that problem the other night at the restaurant."

"That wasn't very subtle, was it?"

"I feel like nothing about you can be subtle. You're too big for that."

"I'll have you know that I can be invisible when I want to. I don't mean that literally, but I'm good at my job, and sometimes, it involves not being seen by anyone."

Orlando couldn't imagine Tanner not being seen, but then, he supposed it was normal in his case. He was always aware of where Tanner was when they were in the same room. The bond wouldn't let him forget it. "Why did you want to get to me, then?" he asked.

"Honestly? I'm not sure. I just wanted to talk to you and make sure you were okay. We didn't have time to talk at the restaurant, since you were working."

"You didn't have to check in on me. I'm fine, and I'm not sure why you think I'm not. Besides, even if I wasn't, how is it your business? We don't know each other."

"But we're kind of friends."

Orlando was surprised at the words. "Are we? Because we've only talked twice, and about nothing friends would talk about."

"Maybe, but you're Quincy's best friend, and Quincy is Cedric's friend. Cedric is my friend, which means that we're somehow friends."

Orlando laughed. "I don't think it works that way."

Tanner smiled.

He was always gorgeous as far as Orlando had seen, but when he smiled, his entire face relaxed, and it made Orlando want to reach for him. Instead, he tightened his hold around his coffee, hoping he wouldn't break his cup, and he stared.

Tanner was still smiling. "I don't know. It brought me to you, didn't it?"

"Because Cedric loves to meddle." Even though Orlando barely knew him, he was sure about that. Besides, he wasn't the only one. Quincy was doing everything he could to convince Orlando to stick around, and apparently, that included throwing him into Tanner's arms.

Maybe Orlando shouldn't have told him that Tanner was his mate. Quincy was his best friend, though, and he didn't like hiding things from him, not even the bad things. Meeting Tanner wasn't a bad thing per se, but it could become one.

Because Orlando had decided he wanted to steal from the mayor.

He knew it was foolish, and he'd decided to retire right after that. He didn't need to rob the mayor, but it was a challenge he wanted to pick up. After hearing so many people say he wouldn't do it, he wanted to prove them wrong. He wanted to show everyone how good he was, but he'd promised himself that once that was over, he wasn't going back to the job.

He had more than enough money to live a cushy life until he died, even though he was only forty-nine. Maybe it was time for him to settle down, and he couldn't think of a better place to do it than in Gillham. That was where Quincy was, and Quincy was the only person who mattered to him.

Well, until Tanner. Orlando still didn't know if he and Tanner would end up together, and he realized that robbing the mayor might put an end to whatever was growing between them. That wouldn't stop him, though. He could survive on his own, even without Tanner. He'd proved that to himself again and again, and this situation wasn't any different. So what if some people—including Quincy—didn't like what he did? Stealing was the only thing he'd ever learned to do, and he was good at it.

"I can go if you don't want me here," Tanner said.

His voice was quieter now, which told Orlando he was hurt, probably at Orlando's lack of an answer.

Orlando didn't want to hurt Tanner. Even if nothing ever happened between them, they were mates, and both he and his cat wanted Tanner to be happy. It would be even better if they were the ones to make that happen. "I don't want you to go," he murmured.

Tanner smiled and said tentatively, "Are you sure? Because you don't seem happy to see me."

"I was just caught off guard, and frankly, a bit bothered by Quincy's meddling. I'm not surprised by it, though, and I know he means well."

"He wants you to stay in Gillham."

Orlando nodded. "And he thinks he can make that happen through you." And he might just be right.

Tanner was relieved that Orlando wasn't bolting out the door. He was intrigued by him more than ever, and he wanted to get to know him. That would be easier to do if he didn't have to run after him.

"Why would he think that?" he asked.

Orlando's cheeks turned pink. "I don't know. I guess he wants to see me fall in love and settle down so he'll know I'm not going anywhere."

"What does that have to do with me?"

"No idea. But that's Quincy for you. Once he gets an idea, he won't let go of it, no matter what happens. I suppose that now that he thinks we make a good couple, he's going to push us together until it happens."

"And Cedric won't be far behind." But that was because Cedric knew Tanner was interested in Orlando.

"I don't know him well, or at all, really. From what I've seen of him, though, I think you're right."

"Does it bother you? We can just be friends." Even though Tanner wanted a lot more than that—he could deal with being friends. It wouldn't be the first time someone he liked didn't want him the same way. The problem was that he'd never felt about anyone the way he felt about Orlando.

"I don't know what I want," Orlando admitted. "Not even from you, or maybe especially not from you. I don't usually live in Gillham."

"Cedric mentioned something about that and about Quincy wanting you to stick around like you just did."

Orlando nodded. "For as long as he's been settled down in Gillham, he's always asked me to move here, too. He wants me close, and I understand."

"But you don't want to stay in one place."

Orlando leaned back in his chair. He looked like he was trying to find the right words, and Tanner wondered why.

"It's not that I don't want to. It's that I'm not sure I'm comfortable living in one place for the rest of my life."

"Why? How old are you?" The answer could tell Tanner whether or not Orlando was a shifter, and he held his breath as he waited for him to answer.

"Forty-nine, so as you can see, I could be here for a long time if I agree to move."

Tanner wasn't sure if knowing Orlando was a shifter helped or made everything more complicated. Beth's idea that Tanner could be Orlando's mate was a definite possibility now, but if that was the case, why hadn't Orlando said anything about it? Most shifters would have, and there had to be a reason for Orlando not to.

Maybe they weren't mates. No matter how drawn Tanner felt to Orlando, it didn't mean there was anything between them, and especially not a bond that would last a lifetime.

"Staying in the same place for hundreds of years isn't a bad thing," he said.

"I don't know. I never really stay in one place for longer than a few months."

"What about when you were growing up?"

Orlando snorted. "That was the worst part. I grew up in

foster care. I moved around often, and I guess it's part of the reason I can't settle down now."

"I can only imagine what growing up in foster care as a shifter was like," Tanner murmured. Until a little over ten years ago, humans hadn't known about shifters. It had to have been hell for Orlando to hide it when he was a child. It was a miracle that humans had never found out about shifter kids. "When did you meet Quincy? Was he in foster care, too?"

Orlando shook his head. "He grew up with his family. We met after I grew out of the system. He was working at a restaurant, and I was looking for food in the dumpster." He said it without shame, without even looking at Tanner.

Tanner was angry over what Orlando had had to go through, but he was also proud that Orlando had managed to survive and had come out of it strong.

"We've been friends ever since," Orlando continued. "He offered me food, and when he moved to Gillham and decided to open his own place, he told me I'd always have a job and home with him."

"Tell me about your job." Tanner had no idea what working at a restaurant entailed, but he was curious.

Orlando's eyes widened, but he schooled his expression after only a moment. "At the restaurant."

Tanner was confused. "Yes. Isn't that where you work?"

"When I'm in Gillham, yes."

"What do you do when you're not?"

"This and that. It's not important. I don't mind working at the restaurant, although I could do without the rude customers."

"I think everyone could do without those, even other customers. Are you planning on leaving, then?" He'd been talking as though he would, and Tanner knew he wouldn't be able to stop him, even though he wanted to.

He wanted Orlando to want to stay. He wanted Orlando to get to know him and to decide he couldn't leave without him.

"I'm not sure. Quincy has been trying to convince me to stick around, but I've never done that."

"Maybe Gillham is the right time and place for you."

"Why? Because Quincy is here?"

And Tanner, but Tanner didn't say that. "Why not? Gillham is a place like many others, and while I know I'm biased, living here is good. It's a small town, but not too small. There are a lot of things to do, and your best friend is here. Most people in town are good, and since you're a shifter, you could even become part of the pack."

"I never told you I was a shifter," Orlando said with a frown.

"You didn't have to. You said you were forty-nine, and you don't look a day over twenty-five."

Orlando blushed again and looked away.

That made Tanner want to reach out and cup his cheek, maybe draw him closer and kiss him. Instead, he kept his hands right where they were, not wanting to startle Orlando and make him run. He was trying to convince him to stay, and kissing him might not be the best way to make that happen.

"But you're human," Orlando said.

"Very much so."

Orlando slowly nodded. "Maybe living in town as a human isn't the same as living here as a shifter."

"Maybe not, although I suppose you should talk to Cedric and Devon about that, since they're shifters. Is Quincy?"

Orlando shook his head. "He's human."

"Has that ever been a problem between the two of you?"

"No. I don't have anything against humans, if that's what you're asking. The main reason I don't know if I should stay in Gillham is that I can't see myself sticking around one place for long."

"Well, I imagine it would make your relationship with Quincy easier. Seeing him every day would be a change, wouldn't it?"

"It's true that I miss him when I'm not around. But is that enough?"

"Why not? You're best friends, and you don't have anyone else important to you."

Orlando arched a brow. "I never said that."

"But you don't. I don't think you're close to anyone you met while you were in foster care. The way you talk, you never had a reason to stick around in one place. Now you do. You have Quincy, and you could have much more, maybe a boyfriend." Tanner frowned. "Or girlfriend." Because he realized he didn't know who Orlando dated.

Orlando chuckled. "You were right the first time. You were right about everything, actually. I'm not close to anyone but Quincy, and if I had the possibility, I'd have a boyfriend."

Tanner wondered if the allusion to the boyfriend thing was obvious. He wasn't exactly offering himself to be Orlando's boyfriend, but he would if he could. "Maybe settling down in Gillham can give you that possibility."

Orlando stared. "Maybe. I guess I'll have to think about it."

"You should. Everyone deserves to have a home, and I can't think of a better home for anyone than Gillham."

Orlando knew what Tanner was implying. He might not realize they were mates, but he had to feel drawn to Orlando. That was why he was here today and why he was saying Orlando might have a boyfriend if he stayed in Gillham.

It was easy to imagine himself with Tanner, settling down somewhere in town, seeing Quincy every day and working for him. Could Orlando do that, though? He'd already decided to retire. He hadn't told Quincy yet, and he wouldn't until he was done. He'd decided to steal one last time, and after that, he would be done. Retiring wouldn't change what he was, though.

A thief.

He would always be a thief, while Tanner was an enforcer. There was no way they could work together, even though they were mates. Orlando wanted them to work, though. Maybe if he never told anyone the kind of job he'd done before retiring, they could manage. Tanner knew he was a waiter, so Orlando didn't even have to come up with a fake job. He and Tanner could get to know each other and date, and he might be able to tell Tanner they were mates.

He would always be lying to Tanner, though.

Orlando had never thought much about meeting his mate, but the few times he had, he hadn't thought he would be lying to the man for the rest of their lives. But that was what he would have to do if he wanted to be with Tanner.

"You look like you're thinking hard," Tanner said.

Orlando forced himself to smile. He didn't want Tanner to understand how much turmoil he felt. "I am. You didn't say anything I haven't heard already from Quincy, but I think that hearing it from someone else who doesn't know me made a difference. Staying in Gillham doesn't sound like the worst thing anymore."

That earned him a smile from Tanner. "It's not the worst thing. I know some people wish to see the world or live in big cities, but I never wanted to leave Gillham. I was born here, and I want to continue living here for as long as I can."

"Won't the council move you?"

Tanner frowned. "You mean because I'm an enforcer?"

"Yes." Tanner hadn't told Orlando he was one, but Orlando had known since the day they met.

"I suppose they could, but I requested to stay in Gillham when possible, and so far, I've been lucky enough to be allowed to do that. Even though I had to change teams a little while ago, I'm still here, and I have every intention of staying here."

He made it sound like a promise, which made Orlando's heart beat faster. He took a sip of his coffee to hide it, but the mug was empty, so he set it down on the table. "I should probably check on Quincy," he said, getting to his feet.

Tanner followed Orlando's lead. "You don't have to worry about him. He's fine with Cedric and Devon."

"I'm not worried about him as much as I'm worried about what they're up to."

Tanner laughed. "You're not wrong there. I've only recently met Cedric, but he's a lot."

They both left the coffee shop, but Quincy was nowhere to be seen. Orlando texted him. *Where are you?*

The answer didn't surprise him. *I brought Cedric and Devon back to the restaurant. Stay with Tanner.*

Orlando scowled at his screen. *Why should I?*

Because you want to? We're giving the two of you space to be together. Get to know him. You know you have to and that you want to.

Quincy knew Orlando better than anyone in the world, although it wasn't like Orlando knew many people, so it wasn't that much of a feat. *I hate you.*

You love me, and we both know it. I'm doing this for you, Orlando. You can't give up your mate just because you're afraid. You have the best opportunity to leave everything behind and have a fresh start. Don't you want it?

Orlando put his phone away without answering. Quincy would fret, but Orlando felt he deserved it after the stunt he'd just pulled.

"Everything okay?" Tanner asked. He sounded genuinely worried.

"Quincy said he and the other two are at the restaurant."

"I see. Cedric and Devon came with me, so I'll have to wait for them to be done to head back to pack territory. Do you have to go to work?"

"Not yet."

"Maybe we could spend some time together."

That was what Quincy and Cedric had been planning. If they'd been here, they would probably be staring with heart-eyes and cooing. Orlando wanted to say no to Tanner just to be contrary, but he wanted to spend time with Tanner more. "Why not? But you know this is what they hoped would happen, right?"

Tanner smiled softly. "I don't see how it's a problem. Unless you don't *want* to get to know me?"

Orlando sighed. "How could I not want to? You're pretty much the perfect guy."

That seemed to startle Tanner. "I'm not perfect."

But he was perfect for Orlando. Orlando didn't say it out loud. He wasn't ready to admit it, not even to Tanner. "We could take a walk in the park," he said instead.

Tanner nodded. "Sounds good."

They crossed the street, walking so close to each other that occasionally, their fingers brushed together. Orlando's breath caught every time as he waited for Tanner to take his hand or link their fingers together, but he never did. He probably thought Orlando didn't like him, or maybe he was giving him space. It would be just like what Orlando knew of him.

Tanner started talking about his family, his sister and his niece and nephew, and Orlando was more than happy to continue listening to him. He tried to imagine what his life would be if he stayed in Gillham and got with Tanner. Tanner came with a family, and while Orlando had no idea how to deal with that, he found that he was curious about it. Tanner sounded like he loved them very much, and Orlando had no doubt they'd be a part of his life, too, if he was with Tanner.

But if he left, he would have none of that. He doubted Tanner would be up for a long-distance relationship, and Orlando didn't think he'd want one, either. If he decided to leave like he always did, he would be giving up his mate.

Orlando couldn't stop wondering what Tanner would do if he found out he was a thief. Orlando knew his luck, and while he always had a lot of it when he worked, in his personal life, he didn't. He wasn't stupid enough to hope that Tanner would never find out the kind of job he had before meeting him. Even if he stopped working right now, that truth would always stand between them. It was too easy to think that Tanner would dump him as quickly as he could. With the kind of job Tanner had, he couldn't afford for his mate to be a thief.

"You're thinking again," Tanner said. He stopped under a tree, a bit away from the path.

Orlando stopped with him. "Sorry. I know I'm not the best date."

Tanner's expression brightened. "So this is a date?"

Orlando hadn't meant to go there, but now that he had, he supposed he should finish it. "I don't know. Is it?"

"I'd like for it to be. It wasn't planned, but that doesn't mean it's not good, right?"

"It's really good." And it was. Tanner was everything Orlando could have wanted from a mate, and even though he knew it was the stupidest thing he could do, he didn't want to give that up.

Tanner stepped closer. When he reached for Orlando, Orlando didn't move away. He didn't want to. He allowed Tanner to cup his cheek, already knowing what was about to happen and unable to say no or stop it. He wanted Tanner to kiss him as much as Tanner seemed to want to, and when Tanner leaned closer, Orlando closed his eyes and let it happen.

Their lips brushed together, softly at first, then, when he didn't move away, more firmly. Tanner wrapped his arms around Orlando and pulled him closer, and Orlando leaned against him. Tanner was strong, and his heart beat under Orlando's palm. It felt steady, and Orlando wondered if Tanner felt that way. He'd be able to know for sure if he and Tanner were bonded.

But then Tanner would also be able to feel how hesitant and worried Orlando was.

Tanner was gentle but firm as he kissed Orlando, and Orlando could only kiss him back. It was the best kiss he'd ever been given, and he never wanted it to end, so instead of stepping away like he knew would be smarter, he wrapped his arms around Tanner's neck and clung to him. Tanner didn't seem to mind or care, and as they continued kissing, Orlando tried to put his mind at rest.

This was nothing. It was just a kiss, and he could still step away from Tanner anytime he wanted to.

Did he want to, though?

CHAPTER FOUR

"**B**ran wants to see us," Sue called out.

Tanner slowed down his running and reached out for the treadmill computer. He quickly took a mental note of how long he'd been running and hopped off the treadmill, headed to the locker rooms to shower.

By the time he left the gym, several team members had already gathered in front of it. They waited for the others to come out, and Tanner's thoughts drifted to Orlando, like they always did when he had time off.

He wouldn't say he was obsessed with the man, but especially now that they'd kissed, he couldn't wait to spend even more time with him. It wasn't the first time Tanner was in love, and he didn't understand what made Orlando so different, but he'd decided to go along with it.

"Do we know what Bran wants?" Lorcan asked as he came out.

"Probably another mission," Jonathan answered. He grimaced, and Tanner understood why.

Jonathan had recently met his mate, and he no doubt wasn't looking forward to spending time away from Cedric. The same went for everyone else on the team. Most of them had a relationship, and spending time away from Gillham would make things harder.

"It doesn't mean we'll have to leave town," he said, trying to reassure the others.

Jonathan smiled gratefully. "You're right. There's more than enough to do in Gillham for now."

But that was coming to an end. The town was clean, and while there were still a few buildings that had to be checked to make sure they weren't dangerous, Gillham was back to its former glory. That meant the enforcers were going to start being sent out on missions again, and for the first time, Tanner wasn't looking forward to it. It was what he'd signed up for when he'd decided to do this job, though.

Once everyone was there, they trudged toward the enforcer's building, where Bran's office was located. The office was big enough that an entire team of enforcers could stand inside and it wasn't crowded, which was what they did when Bran called them inside. Sue sat on the other side of Bran's desk, like always since she was the team leader, and they waited.

Bran tapped his fingertips on top of his desk. "I'm sure that by now you've heard about the string of burglaries that happened in town. I was going to ask your team to investigate, since by now, you don't need to patrol Gillham anymore, but I just got a tip that someone noticed something moving in the mayor's house. It could be related, which is why I'm sending you out."

Tanner straightened. He couldn't believe Bran had assigned them to this investigation. He could see Lorcan bouncing on the balls of his feet and grinning like a loon, and he hoped that whatever they found, Lorcan wouldn't be disappointed.

"Let's go," Sue snapped. She was on her feet again.

"I already emailed you everything we have on the burglaries," Bran called out as they rushed out of his office. "I'll expect a report by the end of the night."

Even though it had been a while since Tanner had done this, he flew through getting ready to head out. It made his heart race, and while there was always a component of not knowing what was going to happen while going on a mission, it also felt good to do something different. It only took them a few moments to suit up in their uniforms and grab what they needed, then they gathered in the shimmering room. Nadha held out her hands, and they made a human chain so she could shimmer them out.

One moment, they were in the enforcers' building. The next, they were in the darkness.

Like always, it took Tanner a moment longer than the others to orient himself. He was human, so it made sense, but it also made him feel like he wasn't quite up to the task. No one said anything, though, and they gathered around Sue, who was looking at her phone.

"How far away are we from the mayor's house?" she asked.

"I'll have to shimmer you there," Nadha answered. "It'll be faster, especially with the fence and the security system that's probably there."

Sue nodded. She put her phone away and faced the team. "All right. Let's not think about the string of burglaries right now. We'll consider whatever is happening in the mayor's house like an isolated case."

"What if it's not?" Lorcan asked.

"We have no way to know, which is why I'm wary of considering the other burglaries. It might not be the same person, and I don't want us to second guess what they're going to do only for them to do something else. So far, the thief in town hasn't hurt anyone. It might be because they don't want to, or because they haven't had the opportunity, since no one was home when they struck."

"Is the mayor home?" Tanner asked.

"Not from what Bran knows. The mayor has been seen in town, dining with the chief of police and a few other people. That's probably why the thief struck tonight. We need to get inside the house and to the thief without him or her noticing, while Bran will contact the mayor."

"The mayor's not gonna be happy," someone in the group said.

"I don't care what the mayor wants. Our job is to stop this thief, whoever they are, and we're going to do that. If you have a problem with it, you can stay out here."

No one said anything, which meant they were all going. Tanner felt better. He didn't want the team to fracture. Still, going inside the mayor's house without knowing anything about the person they were about to face made him nervous. "Do we know if this thief is human or a shifter?" he asked.

"We don't know anything about the thief," Sue answered. She was still frowning. "As far as I know, no one has been able to find out anything about them."

"Then they're probably a shifter."

Sue arched a brow. "Why do you think that?"

"A human would have been seen. Correct me if I'm wrong, but no one has seen the thief. They sneak in and out the houses without anyone seeing them, which to me, points to the fact that they're probably a shifter. There's no way a human would manage this, not every time."

"You're probably right, but I don't want to assume anything."

"It's probably safer for us to assume we're facing a shifter, though."

"All right. Everyone ready to go?"

Tanner nodded, along with the rest of the team. Sue nodded back. "Good. We need to catch this person alive and possibly unhurt. I'm sure the chief of police will want to talk to them, and I'm curious, too. If it's impossible, though, you know the deal. Protect yourself and your team members. You're more important than the mayor's TV or whatever the thief was planning on stealing."

Nadha held out her hands again. Moments later, they

shimmered into the forest. Tanner blinked, looking around, and the first thing he noticed was a huge house. He peeked through the trees, watching the mayor's house. He'd never actually been around here, but then, if he remembered correctly, no one could see the house from the street. The mayor liked his privacy, so the house was set back and the property fenced. Nadha had managed to shimmer them on the correct side of the fence, so it was to their backs, while the house was to their front.

As far as Tanner could see, all the windows were dark. That made sense, since the mayor was out, but it also made him wonder how the thief could see anything. They didn't seem to have a flashlight, which in Tanner's opinion, pointed to the fact that this was a shifter. If they were in their animal form, it had to be a form that saw well in darkness.

"Ready?" Sue asked in a whisper.

Everyone looked around and nodded. They would have waited if someone hadn't been ready, but since they were, they moved toward the house. Tanner took a deep breath, trying to slow down his heartbeat. This was more excitement than he'd seen since the Beasts had attacked Gillham, but for some reason, he still couldn't stop thinking about Orlando.

With every mission, there was always a chance Tanner wouldn't come back. It seemed even more important this time, because he wanted to see Orlando again, and he realized that the *why* didn't matter. It didn't matter if Orlando was a shifter—if Tanner was his mate, and he had a reason not to tell him. Eventually, Tanner would find out, and he and Orlando would fix things.

If they didn't, well, they'd go their separate ways. Tanner would do everything he could to make sure that didn't happen, though. He wanted Orlando, and he was going to get him.

Orlando opened a drawer, peeking inside. The rows of silverware made him smile, but he didn't reach for them. He would have once, but he'd upgraded to jewels and things that were prettier than silverware, even when the forks were silver.

He closed the drawer and looked around. He was still in the dining room, which meant he had most of the house to explore yet. He was looking forward to the bedrooms, which was where the good stuff usually was. Maybe he ought to head upstairs right away.

He was halfway up the stairs, wondering what he would find, when he heard a noise. He froze, his eyes wide and holding his breath. It could be nothing, but he'd learned a long time ago to be careful and to listen to every noise.

It came again. It was like a screech of glass, or maybe someone walking on the gravel around the house. The mayor was supposed to be in town having dinner with the chief of police, along with their wives, so Orlando knew it wasn't them.

A door squeaked as it slowly opened. Orlando looked around frantically, knowing he'd been found. It wasn't the first time, so he knew what to do, but he wasn't looking forward to shifting and hiding his clothes. He didn't usually have the opportunity to come and retrieve them, and if he was going to stay in Gillham, he didn't want to leave anything of his own at a crime scene. It might not lead to him, but he didn't want to take that chance.

Whoever was there was trying to be silent, but Orlando had always had good hearing, and he'd honed it over the years. Just from the sounds, he knew that whoever was here wasn't alone. He'd counted at least three people, probably more. That meant it was an entire team, which pointed to the enforcers.

Orlando's chest felt tight. He'd known that breaking into the mayor's house was a stupid idea, but he'd wanted to show the town what he could do. He'd thought that if he was careful, he would be fine. The house was set back from the street, so no one should have been able to see him. The mayor wasn't scheduled to come back for several hours. Orlando should have had more than enough time to go through the house and choose what he wanted. Instead, the place was crawling with enforcers.

He couldn't stay on the stairs. The enforcers were just entering the house, but they were going to reach him sooner rather than later. He didn't know how many members there were on this team, but he was ready to bet it was enough to surround the house. He would have to be sneaky and careful if he wanted a way out, and for now, it was probably better for him to go upstairs. Maybe he could find an open window and leave that way. It was better than trying to leave from downstairs and being caught.

He finally moved, as silently as he could, which, thankfully, he had experience with. His steps were so light that the stairs didn't even creak under his feet. He moved like a ghost, sighing in relief when he finally reached upstairs but knowing that someone was going to find him soon. He walked into the first room he found, saw it was a guest bedroom, and quickly stripped. Thankfully, the clothes he wore when he was on the job were expendable, even though he didn't like it. It would be hard for anyone to get to him through the clothes since they were all black and generic, but it still felt like a risk he didn't want to take.

Once the clothes were under the bed, he moved toward the window. It was locked, and his fingers trembled as he worked on that. He was distracted, which was the only reason he didn't realize someone had reached upstairs while he was trying to find a way out of the room. He heard a sound just outside, and he shifted in time to see the door open. He didn't even have the time to slip under the bed, so instead, he stayed where he was, sitting on the windowsill in his cat form, hoping that whoever was there would think the mayor had a cat.

The door fully opened, and a tall man stepped in. The house was dark, so it took Orlando a moment to recognize him.

Tanner.

If Orlando had been in his human form, he would have snorted. Of course it was Tanner. That was just Orlando's luck. Tanner was human, so hopefully, it would help Orlando, but Tanner was also an enforcer, so he would know to make sure Orlando wasn't a shifter. There was also the fact that he was Orlando's mate, so he would feel drawn to Orlando, even in his cat form.

This was going to be a disaster.

Tanner's gaze stopped on Orlando. Even though Orlando's cat form was black and he could blend in with the shadows, he was next to the window, so some of the moonlight illuminated him. It was enough for Tanner to see him, even though he was human.

"Shift," Tanner ordered.

Orlando stared. He needed Tanner to think he was a real cat, so he raised one of his paws and slowly licked it.

Tanner growled, which would have thrilled Orlando in any other circumstance. "I might be human, but I'm not an idiot," Tanner said slowly. "You can shift now and come with me willingly, or I can call the rest of my team, and you'll have to deal with them, too. We'll arrest you either way. Do you want it to happen as a human or as a cat?"

Orlando stared. His heart felt like it was about to explode out of his chest, and he knew that if he did this—if he obeyed Tanner's order—nothing could ever happen between them. He knew better than to think he could deal with an entire enforcers team, though. Either way, he was going to lose something—either Tanner or his freedom.

"I see," Tanner murmured.

He reached for the door, and Orlando had to do something. He was dreading it, but he had no choice.

He shifted. He stayed on the windowsill where he was as he and Tanner stared at each other. Tanner's eyes had widened and he was gaping, a sure sign he hadn't suspected Orlando to be the thief.

"Orlando?" he whispered.

Orlando swallowed. "Please. I can explain."

That seemed to snap Tanner out of his shock. He straightened, standing strong and seemingly unmovable in front of Orlando. "You better have a good explanation."

Orlando swallowed. He didn't, but now that he'd shifted in front of Tanner, he might as well explain. "I wasn't going to hurt anyone."

"But you're still a thief. You're here to steal from the mayor."

Orlando couldn't deny that. "I am."

Tanner nodded curtly and reached for the door again. "Don't think that knowing me is going to help. You're a thief, and I'm calling the rest of my team."

"Please," Orlando begged.

Tanner didn't stop. Orlando had to do something, but what? Tanner would hate him for the only thing that came to mind, but if Orlando managed to get out of here, maybe it would be worth it.

"You're my mate," he blurted out.

That did the trick. Tanner stopped moving and stared at Orlando. "What are you talking about?"

Orlando sucked in a breath. "You heard me. It's not a lie, I promise. You're my mate."

And hopefully, that would be enough for Tanner to allow Orlando to leave. Orlando knew it might mean he would never see Tanner again and that he would have to leave Gillham in a rush, including Quincy. He hadn't wanted this to go the way it had, but he couldn't change the facts. Tanner had found him and knew he was a thief. It was a miracle he hadn't called the rest of his team yet and that he was listening to Orlando. Orlando realized it wouldn't last long, but hopefully, it would be long enough for him to convince Tanner to let him go.

Tanner wanted to ask Orlando to repeat himself, but he'd already said it twice. Having him say it a third wouldn't change anything.

Tanner was Orlando's mate.

He'd wanted a confirmation, but this wasn't how he'd imagined he would get it. He'd thought he would be happy about it, but in this situation, he had no idea how to feel. He didn't even know if he could believe Orlando. It might be a lie that Orlando was saying to try to convince Tanner to allow him to go.

Tanner shouldn't even be considering that option, yet he was. If he really was Orlando's mate, he wanted to know what was happening, and he supposed he should give Orlando a chance to explain. This was the worst time and place to do this, unfortunately.

Tanner was going to have to take a risk. It might mean he would be fired as an enforcer, and he didn't know if he was ready to put his job in jeopardy.

Could he risk his mate, though?

Tanner didn't have an answer, and he didn't know what to do. His mate was more important than a job, even than being an enforcer. Hopefully, no other team member had noticed what was happening and Tanner would manage to get out of the situation and save both his mate and his job. Otherwise, he would have to live with the consequences of what he was about to do.

"Shift back," he ordered.

Orlando leaned forward. He was standing in front of the window, entirely naked. In any other circumstance, Tanner would have been staring, but as it was, he couldn't look away from Orlando's face.

Orlando's expression was enough to tell Tanner that he wasn't lying. They truly were mates, and it was tearing Orlando apart to admit it.

It made Tanner angry, but it also told him he was doing the right thing. He wouldn't be able to live with himself if he gave up his mate without even listening to him. That meant they needed time and space away from the other enforcers, and they weren't going to get it now.

"Please," Orlando repeated.

Tanner shook his head. "There's no time to do this now. You have to swear to me that you're going to go to my apartment."

Orlando blinked. "What do you mean?"

"I want answers, and you're going to give them to me. If you're not in my apartment when I arrive later tonight, I'll make sure the enforcers know you're the thief. I'll go after you myself, and I won't let go until you're behind bars."

It would break Tanner's heart, but he could hear the others walking around the house, including those who had been sent upstairs with him. They were exploring the other rooms, and eventually, someone would find him. Orlando had to be gone by the time that happened.

"You still want to talk to me?" Orlando asked.

"I want to know what's going on. Do you have your phone on you?"

Orlando shook his head. "Not on me, no, but it's close by."

"Good. I'll text you my address. It's probably going to take me at least a few hours to get back home. You'll be there when I do, though, and we'll talk. You better have a good

68

explanation for this." And for the rest of the situation.

This was a clusterfuck. It wasn't just that Tanner was Orlando's mate, but also that Orlando was a cat shifter and a thief who had been going around town stealing for the past few weeks. Tanner didn't know how to deal with this or even if he could, but he wouldn't figure it out now.

Thankfully, Orlando didn't ask any more questions. Instead, he shifted after telling Tanner his clothes were under the bed. Tanner quickly grabbed them, opened the window, and threw them out. It took Orlando a moment longer to sneak out of the window, and he stared at Tanner as if expecting something.

Tanner wanted to touch Orlando's fur and find out how soft it was. He wanted to bury his face against Orlando's stomach and forget everything about the situation. Since he couldn't, he gave Orlando a push. "You'll have my address soon. I'll see you at my apartment," he murmured.

Then Orlando was out, and Tanner was staring at him as he made his way off the roof. It was impressive, even though he couldn't see much with the darkness.

"Found anything?" someone asked behind him, making him jump.

He turned around and glared at Lorcan. "Do I look like I found something?"

"I don't know. You're staring out the window. I thought you'd seen the thief."

"Just an open window. I thought that maybe the thief had snuck out through it, but I'm not a hundred percent sure the mayor didn't leave it open. There's nothing here, though."

It was tearing Tanner's heart apart to lie to Lorcan. There was no other way out of this, though, and he soldiered through it, telling himself he was doing it for Orlando.

It was even worse once he and Lorcan went back downstairs. No one had found anything, but they still had to tell

Sue what they'd seen and done. Tanner repeated the lie with his mouth tasting like ash. "I went through the guest bedroom, or at least, I think it was a guest bedroom. The window was open, but that's all I saw."

"You didn't see anyone going through the window?" Sue asked, staring at Tanner.

Tanner prayed she couldn't see right through him like she often did. "I didn't. I'm only human, though, so there might have been someone I didn't notice."

She nodded and moved on to Lorcan, and Tanner relaxed. It looked like she believed him, and while it made him feel terrible, he couldn't stop thinking about Orlando.

He had so many questions, and only Orlando could answer them. Would he, though? Tanner hadn't been lying when he'd said that if Orlando wasn't at his apartment when he came back tonight, he would tell the enforcers what was going on. He didn't care that he would lose his job. Orlando had promised he would be there tonight, and if he broke that promise, Tanner didn't want anything to do with him.

Orlando was a thief, and Tanner was his mate. Tanner had no idea what that meant or how he would deal with it, but he would have to find a way.

"You look like you saw a ghost," Jonathan whispered as they finally made their way out of the house.

Tanner already had his phone in hand, but he didn't dare text Orlando yet, not when Jonathan was right there. "I'm fine. I was just hoping we'd find something more."

No one had seen anything, which meant the thief had slipped through their fingers, or at least, that was what everyone thought. Tanner knew better, and he was sure that if he told the others, they would be angry at him for lying. He would be in their place, but he couldn't do anything else.

He hoped Orlando hadn't been lying when he'd said Tanner was his mate, but also that he had. Tanner didn't want to be mated to a thief, but he wanted to be Orlando's. This entire situation was a mess, and it hurt his head to even think about it.

Jonathan clasped Tanner's shoulder. "We all did, and I'm sure that eventually, we'll find them. Look at it this way, though. It's only a thief, which means that no one has been hurt. No matter how many houses they break into, they're only after material things, not after hurting people."

Tanner supposed he should feel better about that, but he didn't, not really.

Thankfully, it was easy to be distracted, because as they left the house, a car parked in front of it and the mayor stumbled out, indignant and wanting to know what was going on. Tanner took advantage of the confusion to text Orlando, and once that was done, he tried to focus on the job. He might lose Orlando, but he'd do everything he could to keep at least his place as an enforcer.

Orlando didn't want to go to Tanner's apartment. He wanted to run, but he believed what Tanner had said about telling the enforcers that he was the thief if he did. More importantly, Tanner deserved an explanation., no matter how little Orlando wanted to give it to him.

Orlando should have known something would go wrong. He'd decided to retire, had found his mate, and he'd been starting to believe that maybe he could have a tranquil life in Gillham with Quincy and Tanner.

And now, everything was ruined.

He was already back in town by the time Tanner's text reached him. He didn't know where the apartment was, so he used his phone and easily found the building. With every step he took when he got out of his car and walked inside, he could feel the dread and fear weighing down on his shoulders. He was doing this because Tanner deserved an explanation, but he didn't truly believe Tanner could forgive him for what he'd done—both stealing and lying to him.

Once Orlando was in front of Tanner's door, he was faced with a problem. He didn't have the key, and he wasn't about to text Tanner to ask about it. He didn't want to anger his mate more than he already was. Luckily, Orlando was great with locks. Tanner might be pissed to find out how Orlando had gotten in, but Orlando was just obeying orders, which was what Tanner wanted.

And if he wasn't happy, well, he'd just have to deal with it. Orlando knew he'd messed up and that this clusterfuck was entirely his fault, but that didn't mean he would allow Tanner to threaten him and yell at him. He'd made a mistake, and he'd admit it, but it didn't give Tanner the right to treat him like shit.

Making that decision made Orlando feel better, and he snuck into the apartment. He closed the door behind himself and looked around.

He didn't know Tanner well, but he'd expected something modern, with few personal touches. Instead, the apartment was cozy. The furniture was worn but cared for, and there were pictures just about everywhere. Orlando didn't know the people in them except for Beth, but he could guess they were Tanner's family - his parents, niece, and nephew. Tanner was in a lot of them, and he looked happy. Orlando couldn't help but wonder if he was going to take that happiness away.

Maybe he shouldn't have told Tanner they were mates. He'd panicked, and he'd wanted to be sure Tanner wouldn't give him up. Maybe it was selfish, but Orlando had always only had himself to rely on when it came to survival, and this situation wasn't any different.

He didn't want to stick his nose into things that weren't his business and to make Tanner even angrier, so instead of going around the apartment like he wished to, he set his backpack down next to the couch. He would have to be human when he faced Tanner, but he didn't know when Tanner would come home, and he always slept better in his cat form. It was also easier for him to hide if he needed to, so he quickly stripped, put his neatly folded clothes on the couch, and shifted.

The air smelled of Tanner even more when Orlando was in his cat form. He found the spot on the couch that smelled most like his mate, rubbed his face against it, and purred loudly. Then he curled up as tightly as he could, and he closed his eyes. If this was the only opportunity he had to sleep in his mate's space, he was going to take it. Besides, Tanner was one of the few people Orlando trusted not to hurt him if he found him asleep. The other was Quincy, and Orlando winced at the thought of what Quincy would do once he found out about this.

"Wake up," a hard voice said, startling Orlando awake.

He was moving before he could think, rushing to get under the couch. A strong hand caught him, hauling him up, and he found himself pressed against a hard chest. That was when Tanner's scent hit, and Orlando found himself relaxing without meaning to. He even purred, for fuck's sake.

"I have to give it to you. You're cute as hell, and if this was any other situation, we could be cuddling on the couch. I need you to shift now, Orlando. We have to talk."

Orlando sighed and meowed pitifully, but Tanner's expression didn't change. He was still staring down at Orlando, and Orlando suspected he wouldn't stop until he had what he wanted.

Orlando pushed away from Tanner's chest even though it was the last thing he wanted. Tanner put him down onto the couch and, to Orlando's surprise, grabbed a blanket that was on the back of it and draped it over Orlando. It gave Orlando privacy, something he was thankful for. Most people wouldn't have thought about it, but of course Tanner did.

Orlando shifted and wrapped the blanket tighter around his shoulders. He made sure his naked ass was on the blanket rather than on the couch so Tanner could wash it. Then he looked up at Tanner, who was still standing in front of the couch, staring down at him.

"You better start talking," Tanner said. His voice was gruff and his expression hard.

Orlando swallowed. "I'm not sure there's a lot to say. You already know everything."

"I want to start when you arrived here in Gillham. When was it? Did you take advantage of the fact that the town was a mess after the attack?"

Orlando shook his head. "I was already here when the Beasts attacked. I even helped, although I'm not sure how much good it did."

Tanner frowned. "What do you mean?"

"I knew the Beasts were heading to pack territory, so I went there. I'm not good at fighting, but I did what I could, distracting the Beasts and trying to help."

Tanner's eyes widened. "Wait. I remember seeing a black cat during the fight. I was wounded, but you jumped onto a Beast's head."

Orlando remembered it. "A lion shifter. I didn't notice you there, though."

"I was leaning against a tree with a wounded arm. You saved Cedric and his brother."

Orlando hadn't realized that. The fight had been a mess, and he'd done everything he could to distract the Beasts. He hadn't stuck around after he'd jumped onto that lion's head. He couldn't believe he'd been so close to meeting his mate weeks earlier. Maybe things would have been different.

Tanner waved at Orlando to continue. "So you helped during the fight. Thank you for that, but that doesn't change the other things you did."

Orlando sat up straighter. He might be naked, and he might be in the wrong, but he wasn't ashamed of anything. "I know it's a cliché. I didn't start stealing because I was a foster kid. I started because I had no other opportunity. When I aged out of the system, I didn't have anything. I couldn't go to college, and I didn't have a home. I stole before I met Quincy. In the beginning, it was just food. Then other people started relying on me. I was good at what I did, which meant I could steal a lot of food for many people. The food turned into money, jewelry, and I started breaking into houses. I don't keep all the money I steal, though. There are a lot of people out there who need help, and no one is giving it to them."

"But you are."

Orlando nodded. "I am, although I can't say that's the only reason I steal. It's not an excuse, and I know you probably won't believe me, but I'd already decided to retire after today."

"Why break into the mayor's house, then?"

"Because I heard what you and your friends were saying at the bar the night we met. You didn't think I could break into the mayor's house because of security and everything else. I wanted to show you and the others that I could do it."

And he had. Even though he hadn't managed to steal anything and had been found out, he *had* broken into the mayor's house. This wasn't the way he'd expected his last job to go, but maybe it was better this way.

Orlando swallowed. "I know it's going to take you a long time to trust me — if you ever can. But I promise this is it. I'm not going to do it again. I was planning on settling down in Gillham, working for Quincy, and getting to know you. I'm still up for that, but the decision is one *you* have to make. I'm ready to work hard to show you I'm not lying to you and to get you to forgive me. Or I could go. I'll understand if you never want to see me again. But you couldn't expect me to tell someone I barely knew that I was the thief."

Tanner crossed his arms over his chest. "What about the fact that we're mates?"

Orlando winced. "I should have told you sooner, but I knew it would be a problem since you're an enforcer. I was going to tell you after today."

"I don't know if I can believe you or trust you ever again."

Orlando had expected it. "Are you willing to try?" That was all that mattered right now. If Tanner said no, Orlando would leave. If he said yes, though, if he gave them a chance, Orlando would do everything he could to make Tanner trust him and love him.

CHAPTER FIVE

Orlando's phone vibrated. The only two people who ever called and texted him were Quincy and Tanner, and since Quincy was with him right now, it had to be Tanner. Orlando should have been happy about it, but he was mostly annoyed.

Tanner wasn't texting Orlando because he missed him or anything like that. He was checking in on him, trying to see if Orlando really had stopped stealing. Orlando supposed he should be grateful that Tanner was being nice about it and also asking questions about his life and trying to get to know him, but he wasn't. He felt like if he made even one mistake, if he skipped a text or didn't notice he'd gotten one until later, Tanner would arrive to arrest him.

Things weren't going great. After they'd had that conversation at Tanner's apartment, Orlando had left without answers. Tanner hadn't promised anything, not even that he would try to forgive Orlando for what he'd done. Orlando had wanted to give him time, so he hadn't pushed, and now, he was regretting it.

He wanted to know what Tanner wanted. He wanted to know if he should stay or leave. Tanner hadn't handed him over to the enforcers, which was a plus, but where did that leave Orlando?

"Okay, I've had enough. What's going on?" Quincy asked. He sat on the couch next to Orlando and stared at him.

Orlando hadn't yet told him what had happened, and he wasn't looking forward to doing it. Quincy was going to be pissed, probably both at Orlando and at the way Tanner was treating him, but Orlando didn't want to fight with Quincy, too. "Who says anything is going on?" he asked.

Quincy glared at him. "I do. You've been moping since you came back late the other evening. I didn't know what to think, but I was hoping it would change. Instead, every time your phone vibrates, you look a little more down." He paused, hesitant. "You know you don't have to tell me anything if you don't want to, but I'd like to know. I'd like to support you."

Orlando sighed. "There's nothing you can do. And I don't want you to yell at me, which is why I haven't told you."

Quincy frowned. "I'm not going to like this, then."

"You're not. Are you sure you want to know?"

To Orlando's surprise, Quincy reached out and took one of Orlando's hands. "No matter what happened, no matter what you did, you'll always be my best friend. Even if I get pissed and yell at you, I'm not going to abandon you."

Orlando's throat felt tight. "You can't know that. What if I killed someone?"

Quincy arched a brow. "Then I'm sure they deserved it. You're not a bad person, Orlando. You make wrong choices, just like everyone, but that's not going to stop me from loving you and being your best friend. Now tell me. You can't keep this to yourself, not when it's obviously eating you inside."

Orlando sucked in a breath. His eyes prickled, but he didn't want to cry. He wanted to believe Quincy's words, and the only way to see if they were true was to tell him what happened. "I told you I decided to retire."

"You did, and I couldn't be happier."

"Well, before retiring, I wanted to do one last job. I snuck into the mayor's house."

Quincy closed his eyes for a moment. When he opened them, he looked angry, but he didn't yell at Orlando. "I'm listening."

"Someone saw me. They called the enforcers, and a team was sent. Tanner was part of that team. He's the one who found me, and when he did, I shifted and told him we were mates."

"This isn't what I expected."

"It's worse?"

Quincy cracked a smile, which made Orlando feel better. "I don't know. I suppose it depends on how Tanner reacted."

"He told me to wait for him in his apartment. He didn't tell anyone he'd found me and that I was the thief. When he arrived home, we talked. I told him everything, from the time I arrived in Gillham to when I helped distract the Beasts during the attack. I don't know if he's ever going to be able to trust me, Quincy, and I'm afraid I messed things up."

Quincy sighed and wrapped an arm around Orlando's shoulders, pulling him close. "I wish I could tell you everything will be all right, but I can't. I don't know Tanner. I'm sorry this happened to you, though. Have you heard from him since then?"

"He's been texting and calling. Mostly, he asks about my life and myself."

"And that's not a good thing? Because you don't sound happy about it."

"I'd be happy if I didn't suspect it was a way to check up on me and make sure I'm not running around town stealing stuff."

"Well, you can't exactly blame him."

"I don't. I also don't like feeling like a child who misbehaved. He's my mate, not my father. If he wants to check up on me, he should just say it. I understand why he wants to. He doesn't trust me, and I don't blame him for that. But I don't like the way he's doing it."

Quincy slowly nodded. "I see. Well, to me, it looks like you need to talk to him. You're both adults, and you shouldn't have to talk around topics that are important to you. Just get straight to the point and tell him that what he's doing is bothering you."

Orlando had always known this was the only way to fix his problem, but he wasn't sure Tanner would listen to him. Why would he? He didn't trust Orlando, and he had good reasons not to.

Orlando was afraid that by talking to him, he would push Tanner away even more and that eventually, he would lose him. No matter how much he disliked being checked on like a child, at least Tanner was reaching out to him when he did that.

Quincy kissed the top of Orlando's head and got to his feet. "Maybe you should stay home this afternoon," he said.

Orlando shook his head. "I can come to work." He wanted to because it was a way not to obsess over Tanner.

"I don't want you to. I think you need some rest, and you're not going to get it at the restaurant. And don't try telling me you're fine, because you're not. I know you, Orlando. I can see right through your lies."

Orlando swallowed. "All right. I'll stay home."

Quincy smiled. "And I'll bring you food later tonight. We can eat together when I come back, and maybe we can talk some more? I've missed you the past few days."

Orlando hadn't realized he'd isolated himself, and he was sorry he had. He should have told Quincy about this right away. He hadn't wanted to disappoint the two most important people in his life, but Quincy wasn't going anywhere. Orlando was sure of that now, and he was grateful and relieved.

Quincy left after lunch, and as the minutes ticked by, Orlando was more than ever convinced he should have gone to work. He hadn't been looking forward to it exactly, but it was better than staring at the ceiling and wondering when Tanner was going to text him again.

A knock on the door a few hours later made him scramble to his feet. He wasn't expecting anyone, but it was a distraction, and he welcomed it.

Until he opened the door and found Tanner there.

Orlando crossed his arms over his chest and tried hard not to glare. "I wasn't expecting you," he said.

For some reason, Tanner looked uncomfortable. He shuffled his feet and looked up and down the hallway, then finally at Orlando, but only for a moment. "I'd like to talk to you."

Orlando huffed and stepped aside to let him in. "Come in. As you can see, I'm not stealing anything right now. I'm not sure why you had to come here to check up on me. Wouldn't a phone call have been enough?" Maybe Tanner hadn't trusted Orlando to tell the truth if he asked where he was.

Tanner walked in, and Orlando closed the door behind him.

"I'm not here to check up on you," Tanner started.

"Why are you here, then?" Orlando's stomach churned. "Wait. Is it to tell me that you changed your mind and that you're going to tell the enforcers I'm the thief after all?"

Tanner's eyes widened, and he shook his head. "I'm not. I promised I wouldn't tell anyone unless you started stealing again, and I'm not going back on that promise. No, I'm here because Quincy called me."

Orlando suddenly wanted to punch something—possibly Quincy's face. "What did he say?"

"That we needed to talk, and I agree. I never wanted to make you feel bad. And I wasn't checking on you, whatever you thought. I was trying to get to know you."

Orlando had a hard time believing that, but could he really call Tanner a liar after all the lies he himself had told?

Orlando crossed his arms over his chest and scowled at Tanner. Tanner felt he deserved it, so he didn't say anything.

"It didn't feel like it," Orlando said.

Tanner wanted their relationship to start on the right foot, which meant no lies. "Okay, so maybe I *was* checking up on you, at least some of the time. You can't blame me for not trusting that you won't steal again."

Orlando's shoulders slumped. "I never expected you to forgive me or to ignore my past. I know you've already done a lot for me, and if you want to check up on me, then you should."

Now Tanner felt even guiltier, and he deserved it. "But I *want* to forgive you. I don't think that's going to happen until I get to know you and start trusting you."

"And until then, I have to feel like an unruly child. Great. That's exactly how I wanted the relationship with my mate to be."

Tanner hadn't realized Orlando had a snarky mouth until now, but he found he loved it. "Do you think we can sit down?"

"I guess. Quincy knows you're here, so you're kind of his guest."

"But I'm ready to leave anytime you need me to. Just say the words."

Orlando hesitated, and Tanner fully expected him to tell him to fuck off. Instead, Orlando sighed and gestured toward the couch. "Sit down. Do you want anything to drink?"

"Coffee, if you have it."

"I'll start a pot."

Tanner sat on the couch and watched Orlando move around the apartment. He knew his way around it, which pointed to the fact that this indeed was his home, not just Quincy's. Even though Orlando called it Quincy's apartment, it was his, too. He'd welcomed Tanner inside, even though

Tanner hadn't expected it after the way things had been going. He was grateful and ready to do anything to fix things between them.

He didn't say anything until Orlando came back with a steaming mug of coffee. He didn't have one for himself, but he sat on the couch next to Tanner, curling his legs under himself. The movement reminded Tanner of Orlando's cat form.

"What did you want to talk about?" Orlando asked. "Wait. First, tell me what Quincy said. I can't believe he called you without telling me about it."

Tanner took a sip of his coffee, not one bit surprised to see that Orlando had fixed it with vanilla creamer the way he liked it. "He called me to yell at me. I'm not even sure where he got my number, but I'm ready to bet Cedric had something to do with it."

Orlando snorted. "When does Cedric *not* have anything to do with a situation, especially one like this?"

"You're not wrong. I didn't know who it was when I answered, and he didn't give me time to say anything more than hello. He just started yelling that I was the worst mate ever, that I was hurting you and that I needed to stop being a dick."

Orlando sucked in a breath. "I'm so sorry. I swear to you I didn't ask him to call." He paused. "Although I guess my promises don't have a lot of weight."

Tanner shook his head and put down the coffee on the coffee table. "Stop talking that way."

"Why should I? I know you don't trust me. You have every right not to after what I did. I don't blame you for it."

"Stop that," Tanner snapped.

Orlando pressed his lips together and stared.

Tanner hadn't meant to order him around, but he felt like this was the only way Orlando would listen to him.

Tanner took in a deep breath. "I was shocked when I found you in the mayor's house. It wasn't just because I found out you were the thief that day, but also because you told me I was your mate. My sister had mentioned something about that possibility, but I didn't think she was right. I believed that if you were a shifter and I was your mate, you would have told me, especially after we got closer." After the kiss was what he meant, but he didn't know if Orlando would be comfortable with him mentioning it.

Orlando nodded. "I wanted to tell you."

"But you didn't."

"How could I have? I'm a thief, and you're an enforcer."

"You *were* a thief. You said you weren't anymore, though, so unless something changed, it's not a problem."

Orlando snorted. "It's always going to be a problem. Do you really think you'll be able to forget about it?"

"Maybe not forget, but I can accept that it's your past and that I can't do anything to change it. That you've changed and that you're not the same person anymore. That you understand that what you did was wrong, and that since you promised you wouldn't do it anymore, you won't."

"You have a lot of faith in someone who lied to you."

Tanner thought Orlando didn't quite understand what he was trying to say. "We're mates," he started, trying to put his thoughts into an order that would make sense to someone else. "That day, I was angry, not only because I found out you were the thief, but also because you hid the fact that we were mates from me. I've had time to think since then. Your past will never change, and I can either accept it or not, but if I don't, it means you won't ever be part of my life. I don't want that to happen."

Tanner wanted to tell Orlando he'd already started to fall in love with him by the time he found out Orlando was the thief, but he couldn't. He wished he could trust Orlando, and he thought that he would eventually, but it was too soon. He didn't want to expose his feelings until he trusted Orlando more than he did right now.

He wasn't lying when he said that he had to either accept or reject Orlando's past, though. He'd thought about it, and he'd realized he didn't want to lose his mate. He and Orlando could have a kind of relationship Tanner would never have with anyone else, and he didn't want to miss out on that. He also didn't want to lose the man he was falling in love with.

"I'm not sure what you're saying," Orlando said slowly. "How can you ignore my past?"

"The way everyone does when they meet someone they want a relationship with. As long as you promise not to do it again, I can ignore the fact that you were a thief."

"And you trust me when I say I won't do it again?"

"I will in time." That was all Tanner could give Orlando for now.

Orlando sighed. "I suppose I deserve that."

"I wish I could trust you from the beginning, but I hope you understand why I can't. It doesn't mean I don't want us to work as a couple, though. I do, more than anything. And I'm sorry that my texts and phone calls made you feel like I was controlling you. In part it's because I'm afraid you won't keep your promise, but I also want to get to know you. We're mates, and I hope that eventually we'll have the kind of relationship my friends have with their mates."

"But it's going to take some work."

"It is," Tanner agreed. "I don't know about you, but I'm used to hard work."

For the first time since Tanner had arrived, Orlando smiled. "I don't mind hard work, especially when I know the outcome would be good." He paused. "I can't believe you're giving me a chance."

"You better believe it." Tanner decided to take a chance and reached for Orlando. When Orlando allowed him to take his hand, he pulled until Orlando moved closer.

They hadn't kissed since that day in the park, and Tanner couldn't wait to do it again. It hadn't felt right before, not after he'd found out what Orlando was doing, but now it did. It also felt like it was the next step in their relationship and forgiving Orlando and showing him they could work together.

So Tanner kissed Orlando, and when Orlando kissed him back, he smiled against his mate's lips.

Orlando couldn't believe he and Tanner were doing this. He'd expected Tanner to take a lot more time to trust him, and he supposed that even though they'd just talked, he would. Tanner had admitted he didn't fully trust Orlando, but he was trying, which was all Orlando could ask for.

And Tanner was kissing him. He still wanted to kiss him, which was something Orlando hadn't been sure would happen. He wasn't going to say no to that, so he wrapped his arms around Tanner's neck and kissed him back.

He felt himself tilt backward. He didn't do anything to try to stop it, and since Tanner didn't, either, they found themselves falling into a heap on the couch. It wasn't a comfortable position, since Orlando's legs were still twisted under him, but it made him laugh. When he saw Tanner was smiling, he felt better, and he wiggled until he could get into a better position, with him stretched out on his back and Tanner pressed on top of him.

Orlando wanted so much more than this, but this was the best step forward they could take right now. He hadn't thought he would ever get this again, not with Tanner, and he felt like he was in heaven.

Until the phone rang.

Orlando swore and tried to find his cell phone. It was on the coffee table, and the screen was dark. The phone call wasn't for him but for Tanner.

Tanner gave Orlando an apologetic smile and sat up. He didn't move away from the couch, and he kept running his fingertips over Orlando's arm and hand. He took the phone out of his pocket with his other hand and answered. "Yes?"

Orlando was glad he had a shifter's hearing, because it meant that he could hear what was being said on the other side of the phone in the silence of the apartment.

"I need you to come back right away," a woman said.

Tanner straightened, but he didn't stop touching Orlando. "I thought we had today off."

"We were supposed to, but something happened. There's been another burglary."

Orlando's heart felt like it froze in his chest. Tanner's fingers stopped moving on his skin, and Orlando tried to breathe as he watched Tanner. He wanted to tell him he had nothing to do with this, but he didn't want to interrupt Tanner's conversation with his boss.

"Where and when?" Tanner asked.

He took his hand away, and Orlando felt like his heart went along with it. Maybe he was being a tad dramatic, but he thought he was allowed to, considering the situation.

He'd kept his promise. He'd retired after that night at the mayor's house, and he hadn't tried to steal anything else since then. He had nothing to do with this burglary, but would Tanner believe him? He'd just admitted it would take him time to trust Orlando. This was the worst thing that could happen in their already complicated situation.

"Another house in the wealthy area of town," the woman said. "We're not sure when it happened, but it was sometime today. The owners left the house this morning, and when they came back, it had been ransacked. There's no way to know if it's the same thief, but Bran wants us on the case."

"Do you want me to come back to pack territory, or should I head out to that address?"

"Go straight to the house. It'll be faster if you're in town. I'll text you the address, and we'll see you there."

"I'll be there as soon as possible," Tanner promised. Then, he hung up.

Orlando held his breath. He expected questions, so he wasn't surprised when they came. He didn't like that Tanner wasn't looking at him as he asked them, but he understood that, too.

"Where were you today?" Tanner's voice was soft but sounded dangerous.

"I was home the entire day," Orlando murmured. He wished he sounded more sure of himself, but he was terrified.

"What about Quincy? Was he here?"

"Not the entire day, no. He went out for grocery shopping this morning, and he left after lunch to go to work." Orlando swallowed. Maybe it was time to address the elephant in the room. "I was alone part of the day, but I swear I had nothing to do with this. I know you don't have a reason to believe me, and I wouldn't blame you if you didn't. There's nothing I can do but tell you it wasn't me, though. It's your choice whether or not to believe me."

Tanner sighed, and his shoulders slumped. "I have to go."

So they weren't going to talk about it. Orlando supposed he should have expected it. "I understand." He hadn't truly expected Tanner would believe him, so he wasn't surprised. No matter how many times he told Tanner he had nothing to do with this, it wouldn't change anything. He'd lied before, and Tanner was assuming he was lying this time, too.

Tanner got to his feet. "Stay in the apartment today," he said with a gruff voice.

"I wasn't planning on going anywhere. I *didn't* go anywhere. I've been here since last night."

Tanner nodded. "That's good. But continue to stay in. I'll call you as soon as I can."

He reached for the door, but Orlando couldn't let him go without asking one last question, even though he'd just told himself he shouldn't. "Do you believe me?"

Tanner paused with his hand on the handle, not looking at Orlando. "What do I believe?"

"That I'm not the thief, not this time. Do you believe me when I say that?"

Tanner's back was ramrod straight, but his head hung down. He looked defeated, which was enough for Orlando to know what his answer would be, or at least, he thought so.

"I don't know," Tanner said. "I want to believe you, but how can I?"

Without waiting for Orlando to answer, he opened the door and stepped out. The door closed behind him, leaving Orlando alone in the living room. He sucked in a breath, then another, but his eyes burned, and he knew he was going to start crying soon. It was a good thing that he was on his own, but as soon as he thought that, he realized that he had to tell Quincy about this before he found out and accused Orlando of having something to do with it.

There was no way for Orlando to know if Quincy would trust and believe him, but their relationship was much stronger than his relationship with Tanner, so he had hope.

He took his phone from the coffee table, ignoring the cup of coffee he'd made for Tanner. Seeing it there made him want to cry even more, but he had to do this first.

He dialed Quincy's number from memory and waited for him to answer.

"I told you that you didn't have to come to work today, and I don't expect to see your face until I come home tonight. Spend time with Tanner," Quincy said as he answered.

Orlando swallowed. "He just left," he whispered. His throat was painful, and he didn't think he could speak louder.

"For fuck's sake. What happened now?"

"He got a phone call. He had to go to work because there's been another burglary."

Quincy stayed silent, and Orlando could hear the sounds of the kitchen around him. It was oddly soothing, and he realized he'd gotten used to it. Working at the restaurant wasn't his life's dream, but then, he'd never had any. He just wanted a nice life and to be happy, and it didn't matter to him what kind of job he did.

"Where?" Quincy asked.

"The wealthy part of town. Tanner didn't give me the address. It wasn't me, though. I swear." Orlando didn't know what he would do if Quincy didn't believe him. Probably break down and cry before packing his things and leaving town.

Quincy snorted. "I know that."

Orlando sucked in a breath. "You do?"

"You promised you would never steal again, so I know it wasn't you. Why? Did Tanner think you did it?"

Orlando felt like there was something stuck in his throat that he couldn't get rid of, no matter how many times he swallowed. "He said that he doesn't know if he can believe me. He told me to stay here." Maybe so he could come and arrest Orlando after he and his team went over the new crime scene.

"That fucker," Quincy snarled. "Stay where you are. I'm coming home, and we'll spend the rest of the day together. If he tries anything, I'll kick his ass."

"You don't have to leave work for me."

"You're my brother, Orlando. Of course I'm going to leave work when you need me."

Orlando had been trying not to cry, but he couldn't resist anymore. The tears streamed down his cheeks, and he could barely hear Quincy's voice trying to soothe him over the sound of the sobs tearing his chest apart.

He might have lost Tanner, but he'd always have Quincy,

and even though it wasn't the same, it was enough to make him feel like whatever happened, he would never be alone.

Tanner made his way to the address Sue had sent him as if he was in a trance. He didn't understand anything anymore, and he doubted going to work would help. He had to know for sure, though, which was why when he parked, he tried to school his expression so no one would understand he was a mess.

It didn't work.

As soon as he was out of his truck, Jonathan saw him and frowned. Tanner wanted to avoid him, but they worked together, so he plastered a smile on his face. "Hey. Am I the last one?" he asked.

"We're still missing Justin and Nadha. What's going on?"

"I thought Sue called everyone. There's been another burglary."

"She did, and Nadha and Justin will be here soon. And I wasn't talking about the case when I asked what's going on. Something is wrong with you."

Tanner swallowed. He couldn't tell Jonathan that he thought his mate had something to do with this burglary since he was responsible for the others in town or that it broke his heart. "I'm fine, just disappointed we had to come to work because I had plans. Do we know anything about the case?"

Jonathan starred long enough to make Tanner uncomfortable, but thankfully he didn't push. "Sue will talk to us as soon as everyone is here. Come inside. It's a mess."

Tanner frowned. The team hadn't worked on the other burglaries, but they'd seen pictures, and the houses had looked like nothing had happened. Apart from what was missing, it would have been impossible to know someone had broken in and stolen anything. Orlando left the houses as neat as they'd been when he walked in, so a mess didn't sound like him.

Hope rose in Tanner's chest. Could Orlando have told him the truth? Maybe he really didn't have anything to do with this burglary. What were the odds that there were two thieves in town, though?

Tanner sighed. He wanted to believe Orlando, and so far, what he knew pointed to him not being involved, but he couldn't forget or ignore the niggle of doubt in the back of his mind. Until he knew more about what was happening, he had to keep all the possibilities in mind, which meant Orlando was a prime suspect, even though the rest of the team didn't know about him.

Tanner stayed outside until Nadha and Justin arrived. Once they did, they went inside, where Sue and the rest of the team were waiting. Tanner felt like he couldn't breathe, but he did his best to appear normal. Jonathan kept eyeing him as if he expected him to freak out or something, and that was the last thing Tanner wanted to happen in front of everyone. It was bad enough that one of his team members thought something was wrong with him. It would be worse if the others found out about it, especially Sue, who wouldn't hesitate to send him home if she thought he wasn't up for the job.

"I'm sorry I had to call you on your day off," Sue said. They were standing in the entrance, and like Jonathan had said, the house was a mess.

There was a small table on the floor, and everything that had been on it was scattered around. It looked mostly like mail and trinkets, but if this was any indication of what the rest of the house was like, Tanner thought more than ever that Orlando had nothing to do with it.

"The owners came back from a morning out right after lunch, and they found the house in this state. We're not sure what's missing yet because of the mess, but they're going through their documents and anything that could have been stolen, so hopefully, they'll have a list for us soon."

"What do you need us to do?" Lorcan asked.

"Go around the house and see if you can find any clue of who was behind this."

"It doesn't look like it's the person behind the other burglaries," Tanner said. His voice trembled slightly.

Sue nodded. "I agree. The other houses were neat, as if nothing had happened. It doesn't mean it's not the same thief, though. Something could have happened that angered him or her, and this could be their reaction. That's why I want us to go over the entire house. Considering the mess, I hope they left something behind that can help identify them."

They didn't know much about what had happened yet, so Sue sent them on their way. The rest of the house looked like the entrance—most of the furniture had been toppled over, drawers were open, what had been inside thrown around. Even the couch cushions had been pulled off, although the thief had stopped before tearing them apart.

Tanner went upstairs, ready to explore the bedrooms, since that was where he'd found Orlando last time. Orlando had mentioned something about bedrooms and offices being where people usually kept the expensive stuff in one of their text conversations, so if he was responsible for today, too, he'd no doubt visited the bedrooms.

Tanner could hear voices coming from down the hallway, probably the owners going over their things, so he walked into what looked like a child's bedroom. He was pretty sure Orlando wouldn't have looked around this kind of place because who put their jewels in their child's room? But in this case, the room looked like a tornado had gone through it.

Tanner had a hard time believing Orlando when he'd said he had nothing to do with this, but with every detail he noticed, he was more convinced Orlando truly was innocent, at least today.

His phone vibrated in his pocket. He took it out, expecting it to be Orlando or maybe his sister or his mom, but instead, a number he didn't know was on the screen. He frowned as he answered. "Hello?"

"You're a dick," the guy on the other side spat out.

Tanner blinked. "I'm sorry?"

"You know what I'm talking about, Tanner. I thought you and Orlando were working things out, but you accused him of being involved in another burglary? What were you thinking?"

"Who is this?" Tanner asked. It was obvious this guy knew both him and Orlando, and that Orlando was a thief. It had to be Quincy, but Tanner wanted to be sure.

"Quincy, dickhead. Orlando called me crying because of what you just did to him."

Tanner peeked into the hallway, then stepped back into the bedroom and closed the door. "I didn't do anything to him. I got a phone call while we were together, and I had to leave."

"I know you and your team are on the job. There's been another burglary, and you think Orlando did it. You didn't believe him when he told you he didn't."

Tanner sighed. "How can I? He lied to me about the burglaries and the fact that I was his mate. Would *you* believe him?"

"I do. I never thought for one second that he had something to do with this, and you shouldn't have, either."

"That's easy for you to say. You've known him for years. I've known him for only a few weeks, and he lied to me twice about huge things during that time. Look, I'm not saying he did this. The more I see of this, the more I'm convinced he didn't. I can't just brush this off. I'm sorry I reacted badly, but I'm sure he understands."

"He understands? That's why he's crying right now?"

Tanner's chest tightened in pain. "I never wanted to make

him cry or to hurt him. I hope you believe that."

"I don't know what to believe," Quincy grumbled. "But if you truly think he had nothing to do with it, you need to talk to him. He's beating himself up over this, even though he didn't do anything. It's not fair, and if you want a chance to make things between the two of you work, you're going to have to apologize."

"I will." As soon as Tanner was a hundred percent sure Orlando had nothing to do with this. He hoped it wouldn't take long, but unlike Quincy, he wasn't sure he could trust Orlando.

He was going to have to make a decision about this. He could either wait until he found the real thief, or he could trust that Orlando was telling the truth. What he decided would probably make or break his relationship with Orlando, and the thought was daunting.

Chapter Six

It had been three days, and Tanner couldn't stop thinking about Orlando. They hadn't talked again after he'd left Quincy's apartment, and Tanner found that he missed his mate. He was surprised, since he and Orlando didn't know each other well, but he was done trying to fight his attraction to Orlando or trying to stay away from him.

He wanted to go to Orlando and apologize, maybe even grovel since he knew he was in the wrong, but first he needed to talk to someone. Jonathan had been hounding him since he'd realized something was wrong, but Tanner had managed to avoid him until now. He didn't want to anymore, so when Jonathan found him outside the enforcers' house, leaning against his truck and staring at the sky, he waved him over.

"Are you ready to talk?" Jonathan asked.

"I think I am. I just hope you'll take this well."

Jonathan leaned next to Tanner. "Are you going to tell me you're breaking up with me?" he asked, pressing his hand to his chest.

Tanner rolled his eyes. "Very funny. I should tell Cedric about this."

"You can. He'll find it as amusing as I do."

Tanner suspected he was right. He was trying to distract himself by bantering with Jonathan, but it had to stop. If he was going to tell someone about this, he needed to do it now. He would lose the courage if he didn't, but he was terrified that Jonathan would listen to what he had to say then go straight to Sue to tell her about it.

"I promise you can trust me," Jonathan said, his voice softer. "I realize we haven't been on the same team for a long time and that you're probably not sure if you can trust me. Whatever you tell me, though, it will stay between us."

"Even if I know who's responsible for the string of burglaries in town?"

Tanner had expected Jonathan to look surprised, but instead, he slowly nodded. "I expected something like that."

"What does that even mean?" Tanner asked.

"I'm not an idiot. I'm not sure how no one else realized that the burglaries started when Quincy's friend arrived in town."

Tanner was glad he was leaning against his car because the news that Jonathan was aware of what was going on made his knees feel weak. "How long have you known it was Orlando?"

Jonathan shrugged. "Not for sure until you told me just now, but I suspected."

"Yet you didn't say anything."

"Cedric and I discussed it, and we agreed not to bring it up to anyone else, not even Quincy and Orlando."

"Why not? I don't understand why you kept the secret."

"Because even though I'm an enforcer and should want nothing more than for the law to be respected, I realize that sometimes, it's not practical."

"It doesn't have anything to do with this situation, though. You're not talking about someone who's doing it to survive. Orlando has more than enough money set aside to live a cushy life without having to steal again." Or at least, that was what Orlando had said.

"Why is he doing it, then?"

Tanner sighed. He didn't want to discuss this, but he'd been the one to bring it up. "Mostly, he uses the money he gets for the stuff he steals to fund associations that need help.

Usually, it's for homeless kids, especially LGBTQ ones. He was a foster kid, which is when he started stealing. Even after he had enough money that he could stop, he continued because he wanted to help people."

"See? He has a good reason."

"That doesn't change the fact that what he does is wrong."

"You're right. It is, and we should talk to Sue right away. You're not going to, though."

Tanner shook his head. "I can't. He's my mate."

Jonathan sucked in a breath. "I didn't expect that, but I'm not surprised, not with how distraught you are. How does he feel about the situation?"

"I don't know. I haven't talked to him in a few days, not since that last burglary. After the mayor's house, he promised that he was retiring from that life and that he wouldn't steal again."

"What's the problem, then? Do you think he has to atone for what he did in the past?"

Tanner shook his head. "No, but I didn't believe him when he told me he had nothing to do with the most recent burglary. Quincy called me to tell me I was an asshole, and he was right, but I don't know how to fix it."

"Do you believe him now? Or are you still unsure?"

"Honestly? I don't know. I want to believe him, and everything points to the fact that he had nothing to do with it."

Jonathan nodded. "The scenes were entirely different."

"They were, but I'm terrified of trusting him. What if he's lying?"

"What if he's not? Do you really want to ruin your relationship with your mate over something like this? Listen to the bond. Listen to your heart instead of your brain. Your brain will always try to make you see things rationally, but sometimes, they aren't. If Orlando is anything like most shifters, he won't do anything to jeopardize his bond with you. That means that he wouldn't lie to you, not over something this big."

"So you think I should trust the bond between us?"

"I think every mate should. But I understand things are different for you. You're human, and you don't feel things the way shifters do. You have to think about this, Tanner. You said it's already been a few days, and we both know that Orlando doesn't live in town. How long do you think he's going to stick around?"

Tanner hadn't thought about that, and the thought of not finding Orlando in Quincy's apartment when he went was terrifying, even more than trusting his heart to him. "You think he's going to run?"

"I don't know, but I would. If I try to put myself in his shoes, I wouldn't want to stick around to see my mate distrust me that way. You told him you weren't sure you could believe him three days ago, and you haven't contacted him yet, right?"

"Not yet, no," Tanner confirmed.

"What would you think if you were in his place? You haven't contacted him for days. He has to believe that you think he did it. Why would he want to stick around?"

Tanner swallowed. "I have to talk to him."

"You should have a while ago. I wouldn't be surprised if he told you to fuck off, but for both your sakes, I hope he won't. The two of you need to learn to talk, though. Your relationship will be a mess if you don't."

"I don't want to lose him."

"I don't think he wants to lose you, either, but he probably thinks he has. Don't wait to talk to him. Go now, and if you have to, beg him to stay."

"What about the case?" Because no matter how much Tanner wanted to go to Orlando right now, he was an enforcer, and he needed to think like one.

"What about it?"

"Will you tell Sue about this?"

"I won't. I might not agree with what Orlando did, but I understand why he did it. He swore he was retiring, and I believe him. Maybe we could pin all the burglaries on the guy who broke into this last house. Or maybe we'll never find them, and the case will be a cold one. You shouldn't worry about that right now. The only thing you should worry about is getting to Orlando before he leaves town and convincing him you're not as much of an asshole as you appear to be."

Tanner pushed away from his car. "You're right. I'll talk to him, and we can deal with the rest later, once we've made up."

Tanner couldn't think of a situation in which they *wouldn't* make up. After talking to Jonathan, he couldn't help but wonder. What would happen if Orlando refused to speak to him? What if he'd already left town? Quincy would have tried to stop him, but he was angry at Tanner, too, and he might agree it would be best for Orlando to leave. Tanner might have lost the best thing in his life, and he didn't know if he could get it back, but he was going to try.

He had to, because he wouldn't be able to live with himself knowing he'd hurt Orlando the way he had.

Orlando stared at the ceiling of his bedroom. He couldn't do this forever, which meant he had to make a decision, but he didn't feel ready for it. He didn't feel ready for *anything*.

Luckily for him, Quincy wasn't kicking him out. If anything, he wanted Orlando to stay, even now that things with Tanner were a mess. Orlando didn't want to leave Quincy, but he couldn't imagine living in town and having to see Tanner walking around, knowing he'd ruined everything.

The only other alternative was to go, but Orlando wasn't

ready to do that, either. At least not yet. Maybe in a bit, once he admitted to himself that Tanner wasn't coming back, but for now, no matter how hard he tried to snuff it, a part of him still hoped Tanner would forgive him for lying. He hoped Tanner would realize that he really had nothing to do with the last burglary and would come back to him.

He supposed that what people said about hope being the last thing to die was right. He'd never had a lot of hope, but in this case, he couldn't stop himself.

Quincy had suggested talking to Tanner and seeking him out, but Orlando didn't want to push him into something he didn't want, including talking to him. Tanner knew where to find him. Orlando hadn't been at work for the past three days because Quincy had forbidden him to go when he looked like his dog had just died, but Tanner knew where the apartment was. He'd been here. If he wanted to talk to Orlando, he would.

That meant he didn't want to talk to him.

The thought hurt, so Orlando tried not to focus on it. Instead, he thought about Quincy and how happy he was to have Orlando around, even though Orlando was moping. He thought about how hurt Quincy would be if Orlando decided to leave. Even though Quincy had a family, he and Orlando were close. They were best friends, maybe even as close as brothers, and Orlando would miss him. That was the only reason he was hesitating. He didn't want to leave Quincy behind like he had before. Now that he'd retired, he wanted to be anchored in one place, and Gillham felt like the perfect place to do that.

Or at least, it had until Tanner. Maybe if Orlando hadn't met him, he would still want to stay. As it was, he didn't think he could or that he would be able to stand it.

He sighed and rolled to his stomach, dragging his pillow down so he could hug it. The worst part of this was that he understood why Tanner couldn't trust him. When he thought about it, he realized that he *deserved* it. He'd lied to Tanner, both about the fact that they were mates and that he was a thief. How could Tanner believe anything that came out of his mouth after that? He wouldn't have believed himself if he'd been in Tanner's place.

But Orlando had nothing to do with the latest burglaries. He was horrified by what he'd learned, actually. It hadn't stopped at the one Tanner believed he'd committed, and whoever was doing this had no finesse. They tore through houses and stole everything they could get their hands on, including things that had sentimental value to the people they stole from. Orlando always tried to avoid doing that, and he'd certainly never hurt anyone, not like this new thief, who had hit someone upside the head yesterday.

Orlando had hoped the news would bring Tanner back to him since he'd never hurt anyone, but there had been no sign of him. Maybe Tanner believed he wouldn't hesitate to hurt people to get what he wanted. The problem was that Tanner didn't know what Orlando wanted, or rather, he thought he knew better. The only thing Orlando wanted at this point in his life was to settle down, work at the restaurant and make a life with Tanner. It didn't look like he would get his wish.

Orlando had half a mind to go after the other thief. He might have if he were a fighter, but the only thing he was good at was sneaking in and out of houses without anyone noticing until it was too late. He doubted Tanner would believe he didn't have a hand in the last burglaries, so he hadn't even tried contacting him about it. The thought of trying to convince his mate he was innocent and Tanner not believing him made him want to cry, and he'd done enough of that lately.

A knock on the door made him look up. He frowned, not wanting to be disturbed. "I already told you to leave me alone," he said out loud so Quincy could hear. "I don't need food or anything else. I promise I'm fine."

"It's a good thing I don't have food, then," a voice that didn't belong to Quincy answered.

Orlando scrambled off the bed, his heart racing. He was pretty sure he recognized the voice, but he didn't want to believe it. What if he was wrong? He might start crying again if that was the case, and he didn't want to. He was afraid to open the door and see if he was right, so he stood in front of it, his hand hovering above the handle.

"Orlando?" Tanner asked.

It had to be him. Who else would visit Orlando? He didn't have friends apart from Quincy, and that definitely wasn't Quincy. "What do you want?" he asked.

Tanner sounded amused when he answered. "To begin with, for you to open the door."

"I don't know if I can." Because if Orlando saw Tanner again, his heart would break even more than it already had when Tanner told him he didn't want anything to do with him. He was certain that was about to happen, which didn't make a lot of sense because Tanner didn't need to see him to do that, but Orlando was terrified.

The amusement was gone from Tanner's voice. "I promise I'm not here to yell at you or berate you. I'd like to talk to you face to face, but we don't have to if you don't want that. I understand you're angry with me, and I don't blame you for it. I was an asshole, and you have every right not to want to see me."

"Are you about to tell me you never want to see me again?"

"No. But I'd understand if *you* never wanted to see *me* again."

As long as that wasn't what Tanner wanted, Orlando didn't care about anything else. He grabbed the handle and yanked open the door, his heart soaring at the sight of his mate standing in the hallway. Orlando wanted to throw himself into Tanner's arms, but he managed to resist. Tanner might not be here to tell him he didn't want to see him again, but that didn't mean he wanted to be with him. Maybe he just wanted more info on the burglaries. Maybe he wanted Orlando to help him catch the other thief.

Orlando had to keep in mind that Tanner might not want the same things he wanted. He had to focus on what Tanner was saying instead of on his dreams.

He swallowed. "It's good to see you," he murmured.

Tanner nodded. "It's good to see you, too. Can I come in?"

Orlando hesitated. He wanted Tanner in his bedroom, and he'd dreamed about it a few times, but if whatever was about to happen went wrong, he wanted a safe and comfortable place to retreat to. If he allowed Tanner his bedroom, he wouldn't have that. "Why don't we go to the living room?"

"Of course. Quincy left."

Orlando blinked. "He opened the front door for you ."

"I didn't think he would. He's angry at me."

"Did he say anything?" Orlando was surprised, too. He'd expected Quincy to get creative with his knives if he ever saw Tanner again.

"Just that he would kick my ass if I didn't treat you right."

"Well, I'm sure he would try, but I suspect you'd win."

Tanner chuckled. "Probably. Do you want to head to the living room, then?"

Orlando stepped into the hallway and closed his bedroom door. He didn't know what state he would be in by the time he came back, but no matter how many times he told himself not to do it, he found himself hoping.

Tanner didn't look angry. If anything, he looked apologetic and a bit sheepish. Maybe he wasn't here for work after all. Maybe he was ready to give Orlando a second chance.

Or maybe Orlando was deluding himself and would end

the day with a broken heart.

Tanner wasn't sure where to begin. He'd expected Orlando to be sad and angry, but he hadn't realized that what he'd done hurt Orlando as much as it had. He'd expected Quincy to punch him when the man had opened the door to find him on his doorstep, but thankfully, Quincy hadn't. He'd made sure to tell Tanner it wasn't because he didn't want to, but rather because Orlando wouldn't have wanted him to.

Then he'd reminded Tanner that he was very good with knives and used to cutting meat. From the way he'd been staring, Tanner was pretty sure Quincy had plans for his balls, which made him cringe every time he thought about it.

He followed Orlando to the living room. He couldn't stop staring at his mate, and now that Orlando was in front of him, he realized how much of an idiot he'd been. He should have believed Orlando the first time he'd told him he had nothing to do with the burglary, like Quincy had. Instead, he'd decided not to, and he'd possibly ruined everything between them.

The problem was that it wasn't something he could decide. There was so little trust between him and Orlando, which would only change if they gave themselves time to grow it. It wouldn't happen if Orlando pushed him away, which was why Tanner hoped his mate would forgive him.

Orlando gestured at the couch. "Sit down. I'd offer you something to drink, but the last time, you left your coffee untouched."

"I don't want coffee." Tanner was already nervous enough as it was. He didn't need to add coffee to the equation.

Orlando nodded. "That's fine."

He sat on the couch, and Tanner hurried to follow his lead, taking the other side and twisting a bit so he could look at his mate.

"What did you need, then?" Orlando asked. "I heard about the other burglaries. I had nothing to do with those, either, but whoever your thief is, he's escalating. Three burglaries in four days? That's a lot, and not something *I* would ever do."

Tanner had been an idiot to think Orlando would. "I know you have nothing to do with them."

Orlando looked like he couldn't quite believe Tanner. "How do you know that? The last time we talked, you were convinced I was the thief and that I was lying to you."

"That's not quite right."

Orlando crossed his arms over his chest. He was frowning, but he seemed ready to listen to Tanner, which was why Tanner was here.

Tanner swallowed. "I knew you had nothing to do with the burglary as soon as I arrived on the scene. It was nothing like the other burglaries, the ones you were involved in. The place was a mess, with furniture and personal stuff thrown all over the floor."

"So you knew it wasn't me, yet you didn't talk to me. You waited three days."

Tanner rubbed the back of his neck. "I did, and I'm sorry for that. I should have contacted you right away, and Jonathan made sure I knew that when I talked to him."

Orlando cocked his head. "That's one of your team members, right?"

"He is. He's one of my closest friends, and he wasn't surprised when I told him you were the thief."

"You *told* him? Is that why you here? Because you have to arrest me now that you've told someone else?"

Tanner reached for Orlando, wanting to soothe him, but he stopped before touching him. He didn't know if Orlando would allow him to, and he wanted to give Orlando space if he needed it. "No one is going to arrest you, because neither

Jonathan nor I will tell anyone about you. I know my word probably doesn't mean a lot to you after what I did, but I promise you're safe."

Orlando's shoulders slumped just a bit. "Why don't you tell me everything?"

Tanner nodded. "Like I said, I knew you had nothing to do with the burglary right from the beginning. That doesn't mean I didn't have to think about things, though. I know that being with you might become a problem for my career. If anyone ever found out you were a thief and that I investigated one of your burglaries, there could be trouble. As far as I know, though, only five people know about you."

Orlando frowned. "I can only count four—you, me, Quincy, and Jonathan."

"And Cedric, Jonathan's mate. They already knew about it, or rather, they suspected. Jonathan thought it was too much of a coincidence that the burglaries started right after you arrived in town. But they haven't said anything until now, and I don't think they will. I told Jonathan a bit about what you told me about your reasons to become a thief, and he understands. As far as he's concerned, as long as you're retired, he doesn't care about the past."

"That's good to hear," Orlando murmured.

Tanner's throat was dry, but he needed to push on. He wanted to. Not telling Orlando everything would mean keeping the distance between them, and he didn't want that to happen. "I agree with him. I don't care about your past. You promised you'd retired, and I believe you. I needed a few days to put my thoughts into order and realize that even if someone ever finds out about you and decides to fire me, I'll be fine with it. I can find another job. I can never find another you, though."

Orlando stared. "Are you saying you would be fine losing your job because of me?"

Tanner had to be honest, because if they were about to start a relationship, it needed solid foundations, which meant telling the truth. They'd almost lost everything because of lies. Tanner wasn't willing to risk it a second time. "Not fine, but I could accept it if it meant I had you in my life."

Orlando looked like he didn't know what to say.

"I should have trusted you," Tanner continued. "Quincy did, and he was right. And even though I didn't believe you when you first told me you had nothing to do with the burglary, I knew you didn't once I got there. I should have called you, or at the very least, texted you. I should have come to see you sooner, instead of waiting three days. That wasn't fair of me, and I apologize for hurting you."

Orlando waved a hand. "I'm not surprised Quincy believed me while you didn't. Quincy and I have known each other for years. You and I have known each other for days."

It was a bit longer than that, but they hadn't spent a lot of time together during those days. They'd gotten to know each other through phone calls and texts, but there had been too much standing between them. Tanner had been hurt because of what Orlando had done, and Orlando had believed Tanner was checking in on him. And he *had* been, but that wasn't the only reason he'd called Orlando. All of that was behind them now, or at least, Tanner hoped so. There was only one way to find out.

He cleared his throat. "I'll understand if you don't want to see me again. I deserve it after what I did. It was a huge fuck up, but if you're willing to give it to me, I'd like a chance to show you that I can be a good guy."

"I already know you're a good guy."

"That I can be a good mate, then. You deserve it."

Orlando was still staring. "Are you saying that you still want me after everything that happened between us?"

"I've never stopped wanting you. That's one of the reasons

I needed to put distance between us. I didn't want to be influenced by the attraction I feel for you or the bond. Resisting it hasn't been easy, not when it wanted me to believe whatever you said, to find you and drag you into my bed. But I know the bond has nothing to do with my decision to trust you. I realize you owe me nothing and that it's going to take a long time for you to forgive me. I'd just like a chance to show you how much you mean to me and what can happen between us."

Tanner fully expected Orlando to tell him to take a hike, or maybe, if he was feeling generous, agreeing to give him a chance. What he didn't expect was Orlando to scramble to his knees and throw himself at him.

Orlando wrapped his arms around Tanner's neck and pressed his body against him. Tanner could only do the same and hold Orlando close as he kissed him. He hoped it meant Orlando forgave him, but he needed to know for sure. "What does this mean?" he asked in a whisper, afraid to break the moment.

"That I don't care about the past. We have a lot of work to do, but we'll do it together, and that's all that matters." Then, Orlando kissed Tanner again, and Tanner stopped resisting.

He had what he'd come for. He had his mate in his arms, and Orlando was willing to give them a second chance. They could talk again later, as many times as they needed. For now, Tanner wanted Orlando close, and he suspected the same went for Orlando.

Orlando had wanted this to happen since the first time he'd seen Tanner, but he hadn't believed it would. There was too much between them, too many things they needed to get over. Tanner *was* kissing him, though, and from the feel of it, he wanted more.

Orlando would be more than happy to give it to him. He wanted to give Tanner everything he could ever want.

"I'm not ready to bond," Tanner murmured.

Orlando froze. He wasn't sure how to answer, but he knew Tanner needed reassurance from him. "It doesn't matter. We don't have to bond. It doesn't mean I'm going to leave or start stealing again. I made a promise to you, and I intend to keep it. I swear."

Tanner pushed back and shook his head. "That's not what I was talking about. I know you'll keep your promise, and I shouldn't have doubted you before."

"It was only natural that you did. You didn't know me. You still don't." And Orlando didn't want it to be a problem between them.

"I don't have to know you to know you'll keep your promise, if not to me, to Quincy. And I don't want to keep pushing you away. Even if something happens and I have to resign from my job or if I'm fired. You're more important than a job. I can find something else, but I'll never find another you."

"Because I'm your mate."

Tanner kissed Orlando's nose. "Because you're you. It doesn't have anything to do with me being your mate. I kept you at arm's length because I didn't want my life to change, and it was easy to use what you did as an excuse. I'm done being an asshole, though. You deserve to be happy as much as anyone else, and since you want me in your life, I'll do everything I can so you won't ever regret it."

Orlando's heart might just be about to explode from happiness. "I only need you to be yourself."

Tanner snorted. "It hasn't worked well until now."

Orlando didn't want to talk about this anymore, but he wanted Tanner to know one thing. "I don't blame you for being wary. I would have been in your place, too, so I understand. I want us to leave this behind, though. You believe I had nothing to do with the latest burglaries and that I won't steal again. That's all I need and want to hear. Now, I want to focus on our relationship, and only on that. I never expected to find my mate or make a life in Gillham, but I know I'm not going anywhere."

"I'm not, either."

Then Tanner kissed Orlando again, and Orlando hoped they were done talking, because he'd wanted to get his hands on Tanner's body since they'd met, and it was time to finally do it, dammit.

Orlando wrapped his arms around Tanner's neck and pulled until Tanner moved and pressed his body on top of Orlando's. Orlando opened his legs even more, hooking his feet around Tanner's thighs just in case he decided to stop. Orlando didn't want to, and he would make sure Tanner knew it.

"What about Quincy?" Tanner asked as he traced a path down Orlando's neck with his lips.

It took Orlando a moment to understand what he was saying. "Why do you want to know about Quincy?"

"Because we're on his couch, and I don't want him to kick my ass."

Orlando laughed. "I'm pretty sure he'd be happy to see we made up. I don't know where he is, though. You're the one who talked to him when you arrived."

"He said he was going to the restaurant." Tanner pushed Orlando's t-shirt up until it reached his armpits. "How long do we have?" He kissed Orlando's chest.

That made it hard to think—or breathe. "I don't know. He probably knows what we're up to." And he wouldn't be happy to find them on the couch.

Orlando groaned. He didn't want to stop what he and Tanner were doing, but it would be better than having Quincy kick his ass for having sex on his couch. "We should head to my bedroom." They shouldn't have left it to begin with, but Orlando hadn't known why Tanner was here, and he'd wanted to have a place to retreat if things went the wrong way.

They hadn't, thankfully, and now more than ever, he needed to feel close to Tanner. If they could do it while being naked, well, he wasn't going to protest.

Tanner hauled himself off the couch and offered Orlando his hand. Orlando took it, allowing Tanner to pull him up and smiling when Tanner dragged him into his arms. "We're going to fall back on the couch if we start kissing again," Orlando said when Tanner kissed his neck. He couldn't stop himself from tilting his head to give him easier access, though.

"Right," Tanner said as he straightened. "Let's go." He took Orlando's hand and pulled him along.

Orlando would have gone anywhere Tanner took him, but he was glad it would be his bedroom. He didn't even care that it was a mess of dirty clothes and empty energy drink cans. He doubted Tanner would notice any of that.

Orlando pulled his t-shirt off and dumped it on the floor as soon as the door was closed behind them. He was grateful he wasn't wearing shoes or socks, because that meant it was just as easy to get rid of his jeans. Before he could dump his underwear, too, Tanner caught his hand and dragged him forward—right into his arms.

"Why are you in such a rush?" he asked.

"Because I've been dying to get you in my bed."

Tanner arched a brow. "And?"

Dammit. He saw too much. "And I'm afraid this is the only time we'll do this, and I want to enjoy it as much as I can. I'm scared you'll change your mind."

"I won't. I can't promise we'll never fight, but I'm not going anywhere, just like you aren't."

Orlando heard the words, but the niggle of doubt stayed in

the back of his mind. He wouldn't get rid of it anytime soon, but he hoped that eventually it would disappear. In the meantime, he had things — or in this case someone — to do.

Orlando reached for Tanner's t-shirt and pushed it up until Tanner got the idea and tugged it off his body. "Okay, you're not leaving, and neither am I. Does it really mean we have to take it slow, though?" he asked.

Tanner's laugh was rough. "No. As long as you realize we'll have the opportunity to do this time and time again, we can go as fast or slow as you want." He hesitated. "But we're not bonding yet."

"That's fine." And it was. Even though Orlando was afraid Tanner would leave eventually, he didn't want that to be the reason behind their bonding. He wanted to be sure of what was between them before they took the final step in their relationship. "But you're not naked enough." Waiting to bond didn't mean they had to wait to have sex.

Tanner's chest shook with laughter when Orlando touched it. It was enough for Tanner to suck in a breath, and Orlando used his surprise to push him onto the bed. Tanner's legs dangled off, which was great for Orlando's plans, because it made it easy for him to untie Tanner's boots and pull them off his feet. Tanner's socks were next, but when Orlando pulled on Tanner's jeans, they were stuck.

He looked up and glared at Tanner. "Mind helping?"

Tanner looked lazy and like he belonged in Orlando's bed. "I thought you were doing everything on your own."

"I can do it, but only after I get your jeans off. Unfasten them before I tear them from your body."

Tanner shuddered and obeyed.

Orlando wondered how Tanner would react if he used his nails on him, so as soon as Tanner's jeans were on the floor, too, he raked them up Tanner's legs.

Tanner shuddered again. Orlando grinned and reached for

his nightstand. Once he grabbed the lube, he threw it onto the mattress, then climbed on top of the bed—and Tanner, who, unfortunately, was still wearing his underwear.

A purring sound came out of Orlando's throat without him meaning to make it. He pressed his lips together, but thankfully, Tanner didn't say anything. Instead, he reached for Orlando, but Orlando wasn't yet ready to give in. He moved back, grinning, and hooked his fingers into the elastic band of Tanner's underwear. This time he didn't have to ask for Tanner to help. He raised his hips, and Orlando dragged the underwear down his legs.

Then Tanner was naked. Orlando had known Tanner was hard for him, but seeing it without anything covering him made his mouth water. He raked his nails up Tanner's inner thigh, causing Tanner to shiver again, especially when Orlando reached his balls. He made sure to keep the touch light once he was there because he didn't want to hurt his mate, but it was something they might want to explore eventually.

"You're not naked yet," Tanner croaked.

Orlando rolled his mate's balls in his hand. "And you want me to be?"

"I want to fuck you, and that'll be easier if you're naked." He grinned. "I can tear your underwear off your body if you don't want to help."

"That won't be necessary." Orlando rose on his knees and pushed his underwear down, then he flopped onto his back and wiggled them off his legs. Since he was there, he grabbed the lube and opened it, too.

He could feel Tanner's gaze on him, but he didn't look at his mate. Instead, once the lube was open, he rose to his knees again and slicked his fingers. He dumped the lube back on the mattress and reached behind himself as he also leaned down and wrapped his lips around Tanner's cock.

He knew it was stupid, but he wanted to show Tanner he

was here for him. He wanted to show his mate that he truly wasn't going anywhere, that he was his, that he would take care of him.

So he did. He was more careful and thorough with Tanner than he was with himself because he wanted to feel what they were about to do later still. When it came to Tanner, though, Orlando took his time, sucking and licking him until he could feel him shudder under his touch. The sounds Tanner made drove Orlando crazy, and as soon as he was prepped enough that it wouldn't hurt more than he wanted it to, he rose and straddled Tanner.

Tanner's hands went to Orlando's hips, but he didn't try to push him down and force him into anything. He allowed Orlando to move at his own pace, which made Orlando fall in love with him just a bit more. He reached under himself to take Tanner's cock.

Orlando had to swallow before he could continue. He looked at his mate as he lowered himself onto him, never looking away. He didn't think he could have even if he'd tried. Tanner's expression twisted as he pushed inside of Orlando, but their gazes were locked.

Orlando stopped moving once his mate was entirely inside of him. It had been a long time since he'd done this because he didn't trust easily. The fact that he was doing it with Tanner, with his *mate*, made it all the more special.

Tanner's fingers dug into Orlando's hips as Orlando started moving. He felt full and on the brink of pleasure already, so he didn't take it slow. He moved up and down, moaning and touching every inch of Tanner's skin he could reach, needing more. It was out of reach, but he didn't mind the chase, especially if it was short.

It turned shorter when one of Tanner's hands moved around Orlando. He felt Tanner's fingertips touch the spot where Tanner's dick thrust inside him. Tanner gently tugged, making Orlando groan. Orlando reached for Tanner, who sat up and wrapped his arms around Orlando's body.

Then he nipped Orlando's neck.

Orlando whimpered as he came. He couldn't believe Tanner hadn't even touched his cock, but the biting had been enough to push him over the edge. Tanner held him and continued to fuck him until he shuddered against Orlando's chest.

They were wrapped around each other, both trying to slow down their breathing. Orlando wasn't ready to let go, not yet, maybe not ever. He would do all he could to keep Tanner in his life, and he would promise that again and again until Tanner believed him.

CHAPTER SEVEN

Tanner had been thinking about bonding—a lot. He felt he hadn't been able to think about anything else since he and Orlando had gotten together. He still had doubts about bonding with Orlando, but he suspected they wouldn't fade until he made his decision. There were always pros and cons to every big decision, and this was just about the biggest he'd ever made.

He wanted to bond with Orlando.

He'd taken his time to think about it, and he realized some people would think it was too soon. He and Orlando had been together, really together, for only a month and a half. They'd been working things out, and Tanner couldn't have been happier.

He rolled his head on the pillow to look at Orlando. His skin still glistened with a sheen of sweat after they'd made love, and when he noticed Tanner looking at him, he smiled. Tanner couldn't help but smile back. He always did when Orlando smiled at him, and Tanner thought he would even when they were both old with white hair and creaky bodies.

Tanner was in love with Orlando, and the bond between them was strong, even though they hadn't bonded yet. He would never get rid of it, and he didn't want to. If anything, he wanted it to be stronger.

"What are you thinking about?" Orlando asked as he rolled to his side, facing Tanner.

Tanner grabbed Orlando's hips and pulled him close until their bodies touched. He rolled sideways, too, plastering them together.

Orlando laughed. "I might be a shifter, but I still need some time to rest between one fuck and another. Give me half an hour."

Tanner couldn't do anything but stare. Orlando had been living with him unofficially since they'd gotten together. He still had some of his things in Quincy's guest room, but more and more of his things had drifted over to Tanner's place. Everywhere Tanner looked, there were little signs of Orlando, and he loved it. They hadn't talked about it, but he was starting to suspect they didn't need to.

Or maybe they did, and asking Orlando to bond with him was the first step in that conversation. Or maybe the last. He didn't care what order they did this in, as long as they did it.

Orlando frowned. "You're starting to worry me. What's going on in that head of yours?"

"I want us to bond," Tanner said.

Orlando's eyes widened. "What?"

"You heard me." Tanner pulled Orlando even closer. "I want us to bond. We've been walking around the issue since we got together, and I think it's time to stop. You don't have to say yes if you don't want to, but I've made my decision, and I won't change my mind."

"Of course I want to bond with you. I'm just not sure you understand the implications."

Tanner rose on his elbow. "I think I do. I talked to Jonathan and Cedric. I talked to other mated couples on my team. They were honest about what bonding with someone meant, and I know what it entails. If we do this, I'll be able to feel you in my mind and my heart, and you'll feel me. We won't ever be able to break the bond. I'll be able to walk away from you if I really want to, but you won't. I don't think that's fair, but there's nothing I can do to change it. What I can do is love you and cherish you for the rest of our lives."

Orlando looked like he was about to cry, and Tanner hoped it would be good tears and not bad ones. "You really did think this through, didn't you?" Orlando asked.

Tanner nodded. "I always do when it's an important decision. We can wait if you want, but I know that you're it for me. I'll love you for the rest of my life, and I hope you'll do the same. I don't see a good reason to wait, even though we've only known each other a little over two months. I already know I love you. I already know I'll never stop loving you."

Orlando threw his arms around Tanner's neck and pulled him down on top of him. Tanner was always careful because he was bigger than Orlando, but when Orlando wrapped his legs around Tanner's waist, Tanner couldn't move anymore.

"I thought it would take you much longer to agree to this," Orlando said.

Tanner rolled them so he would be under Orlando. "How could I not want to be bonded to you? You're perfect."

Orlando snorted. "I'm pretty sure that's a lie."

"We're perfect for each other, then." And they were.

Orlando didn't have to tell Tanner he wanted to bond, too. The way he reached for his neck with one shifted finger was enough of an answer. Seeing only one finger shift was fascinating, but now wasn't the time to ask questions about it. Tanner's attention was on the blood that beaded from the scratch Orlando had created on his own skin. He knew he had to drink it, and while the thought made him wrinkle his nose, he didn't hesitate.

He pulled Orlando down, pressing his lips against his skin. The taste of blood in his mouth felt wrong, but also right. He gently sucked on the wound, wondering how much blood he needed to drink.

A flash of pain in his neck made him jolt, but he realized that Orlando had bitten him. He hadn't warned him, which Tanner was grateful for. He was pretty sure he would have freaked out at least a bit at the thought of Orlando gnawing on his neck.

That wasn't what this was about. It was about their love and their relationship, about what they shared. It was about making what they had complete, and Tanner sucked on the scratch, wanting more and hoping it was the right way to do this.

With every mouthful of blood he drank, he could feel Orlando closer, not physically but mentally. They weren't quite becoming one, but Tanner would always carry a piece of Orlando in him, which was all he wanted.

He knew the exact moment the bond between them was complete. He'd never felt anything like it, and he never would again. It was the bond two mates shared, and it would link him and Orlando for the rest of their lives.

Orlando was there, in every one of Tanner's thoughts, in every move he made, and it was magical. It was nothing like Tanner had expected because it was *better*. Tanner knew Orlando was relieved, over the moon happy, but also a bit hesitant and confused. He didn't know why Orlando felt that way, but it was enough for him to know how to take care of his mate.

Tanner gently licked the scratch on Orlando's neck and leaned back. It would heal, so no one would know Orlando was bonded, but maybe Tanner would eventually manage to put a ring on Orlando's finger. There was time to talk about that, though. Maybe once Orlando was more secure in their relationship, Tanner would ask.

Orlando's weight became heavier on top of Tanner, but Tanner didn't mind. He wanted to be as close to his mate as he could right now, which made this position perfect.

"You're wearing my bite," Orlando murmured.

Tanner reached up. Sure enough, there was a new scar on his neck, the scar he would wear proudly. His thoughts went back to the ring he'd been thinking about, but he pushed it away. Now wasn't the time. "I like it," he told Orlando.

Orlando kissed it. "I like it, too."

Tanner brought Orlando's face closer and kissed him on the lips. Whatever Orlando had said about needing half an hour, it didn't look like it would be a problem.

Tanner's phone rang. He groaned, dropping his head back onto his pillow. Orlando chuckled and rolled off him, grabbing the phone from the nightstand and handing it to him. When Tanner saw it was Jonathan, he didn't want to answer, but he did. "Please tell me I don't have to come into work today."

"Why? Do you have something better to do?"

"Actually, I do." Tanner looked at Orlando, who looked like he belonged in his bed. "I can ask for a day off for bonding with my mate, right?"

"Really?"

"Really." And it was partly thanks to Jonathan, who had helped Tanner pull his head out of his ass.

"Well, congrats. But I wasn't calling you for the job, at least not entirely. It's not our case, but I just heard from a friend that they found the thief."

Tanner sat up. "What do you mean?"

"A team was called to the scene of an ongoing burglary last night. They tried to arrest the thief, but he ran and died when he fell off the roof. Apparently, he was a Beast we hadn't managed to find. He'd been hiding in empty houses and stealing everything he could from them. He's also the guy who hit that victim upside the head. Since he's dead, he can't declare that he didn't enter all the houses that have been broken into recently. They're putting everything on him."

Tanner relaxed. Jonathan wasn't saying it, but Tanner knew what it meant. They'd found the thief, and Orlando was free of suspicions. "Thanks for calling."

"I thought you and your mate would want to know about this as soon as possible. Have fun, but remember that we're meeting at the bar tonight. Cedric hasn't been able to shut up about seeing Orlando again."

They hung up, and Tanner threw his phone on the nightstand. Then he stretched out on his back and pulled Orlando into his arms. "They found the thief," he explained.

"You mean the other thief?"

"I mean the only one in town. The guy is dead, so he can't explain that he didn't break into all those houses. Everything is being put on him, so you're as innocent as I am."

"That's good. I know you were worried that it might impact your job if someone found out about me."

"But I would have chosen you."

Orlando kissed Tanner's chest. "That doesn't mean I was happy about you having to do it. This is a relief, although I do feel a bit guilty."

"Don't be. The guy hit someone, causing them a concussion. He was a Beast, which means he was here during the attack on the town. I doubt anyone will care that he only broke into some of those houses and not all of them. *I* certainly don't."

And maybe it made Tanner selfish, but he didn't care.

"You don't have to go to work, then?" Orlando asked.

Tanner shook his head and squeezed him harder. "I'm yours for the rest of the day." And the rest of his life.

Orlando grinned and twisted until he straddled Tanner's hips. "Good. I have plans."

Tanner was more than happy to give in and do everything Orlando wanted. He wanted to do it forever, and he would.

They were bonded, and neither of them was going anywhere. They would make their home in Gillham, and they would be happy. Now that the Beasts had been taken care of, Gillham was safe and as beautiful as it had been before. This felt like a new start for the town, and now, for Tanner and Orlando, too.

YOU MAY ALSO ENJOY THE FOLLOWING FROM EXTASY BOOKS INC:

Perfectly Imperfect
Catherine Lievens

Excerpt

Josiah stared at the piece of paper in front of him on the desk. It was supposed to have a list of names written on it, but instead, it was empty. He had no candidates to fill his beta spot, and he knew better than to think he ever would, at least when it came to the coyotes.

So far, he hadn't been doing a good job as the new alpha. He barely knew where to start, but he did know he needed a beta. The problem was that no one wanted to work with him.

He snorted to himself and leaned back in the chair that had once belonged to his father. It wasn't only that no one wanted to work with him. No coyote respected him, either, which made things even harder. He didn't know how to break through that, or even if he could.

Maybe he shouldn't have accepted the alpha position. He understood why the council had needed him, and if it kept the humans off their back for a while, he was willing to continue, but he doubted he could actually do this. Shifters had to respect their alpha, and they didn't when it came to him.

He couldn't blame them. How could anyone respect him after what his father and his brother had done and the way they'd treated him in front of everyone? They believed what their old alpha had told them, which was that since Josiah was a carrier, he wasn't fit to become anything, least of all an alpha. It just wasn't done anywhere in the forest.

But things were changing. Josiah had never imagined he would be the first alpha carrier in the forest, yet here he was. In a few years, he wouldn't be the only one anymore. In the meantime, though, the position was unique to him, and he didn't know what to do.

He could ask for help. The council and Thomas, the badger alpha, had offered to help any way they could. Josiah wasn't proud enough to say no, but he didn't think they could do anything in this situation. He needed a beta, and it would be better if that beta was a coyote. Of course, it would be a problem if the band respected his beta more than they respected him, but he supposed he would deal with that problem if it ever happened. In the meantime, he was trying to deal with the band on his own, and they were ignoring him.

That was going to become a problem soon, and Josiah had no idea how to solve it.

He grabbed his cell phone from the desk and opened the messaging app. I want to go home, he wrote.

Nico's answer came only a few moments later as if he'd been waiting with his phone in hand. It was surprising since he was training with his father to become the next alpha. His twin brother had thrown him and their father for a loop when he'd decided to step down from the role and move in with the badgers, but Nico was more than happy to take Chris's place.

Isn't that what we all want? Nico's answer was.

Josiah frowned. I thought you wanted to become the next alpha.

I did. I do. It's more complicated than I thought, that's all.

Tell me about it. Nico had been there every step of the way for Josiah, and Josiah was grateful. Now that they didn't live together anymore, he missed his best friend something fierce. He wished Nico could move in with him and maybe become his beta, but it just wasn't possible.

What's going on?

Josiah sighed. He didn't want to dump all his problems on Nico, especially not since Nico seemed to have his own. Nothing much.

Bullshit. Talk to me, Joe.

Josiah glared at the screen. I told you not to call me that.

Fine. Talk to me, Josiah.

Josiah rolled his eyes. I still haven't found a beta. If he couldn't tell Nico about this, and who could he tell? Thomas would listen to anything Josiah had to say, but he didn't want to burden the older alpha. The man already felt guilty enough that he'd pushed Josiah to accept this role. He wasn't wrong, though. Josiah wouldn't have accepted if Thomas hadn't asked. But Josiah owed Thomas everything, and if there was even one thing he could do to thank the man, he would do it.

Even if the thing was becoming alpha to people who hated him.

Has no one volunteered? Nico asked.

You know better than to think anyone would.

The three dots on the screen danced as Josiah waited for Nico to answer. He startled when his phone started ringing instead of a text appearing on the screen, but since it was Nico, he answered. "You should be working," he said.

"Yes, well, I'm not the only one. What's going on?"

"Nothing different than what was already going on before."

"Are they still ignoring you?"

"On the good days. On the bad ones, they snap at me and tell me I should never have become the alpha."

"They should be punished for that."

That word made Josiah cringe because it reminded him of his father. Nico wasn't wrong, though. "And who's going to punish them?"

"You're the alpha. You ought to do it, or at the very least, order it."

"Me and what army? You know they're not going to care. They don't respect my authority, and I don't think they ever will. My father saw to that."

"Your father was a dick." Nico sounded fierce.

Josiah's heart swelled. Once, he hadn't thought he would ever have a best friend. Hell, he'd thought he wouldn't be alive past his twenties. His father and his brother had abused him, and there had been nothing he could do about it. But he'd survived, and here he was, at twenty-three years old, a carrier and an alpha.

This was nothing like the life he'd expected to have, but in many ways, it was better. He wasn't alone anymore. He had people he cared about and who cared about him. He didn't have a lover, and he wasn't planning on finding one anytime soon, but he was young. He had time for that. Right now, he needed to focus on the band. If he didn't manage to get them under control, the humans would step in, and no one wanted that to happen.

Maybe that was what Josiah should tell the coyotes. He could make sure they knew what was going to happen if they didn't listen to him. He didn't understand why they didn't. Both his brother and his father had been abusive, and not only to him. They'd been bad alphas, and he didn't understand how the band wasn't relieved that they were gone and happy to have a decent alpha.

Not that it took a lot to be a decent alpha considering whose shoes Josiah was filling, but he supposed that doing nothing was better than what his brother and his father had done.

"I guess we should be grateful they're not making too much of a fuss," he told Nico.

"They don't want the council to know they don't accept you."

"I don't want the council to know, either. You know what's

going on. We can't afford to gather even more attention from the humans." The band was already in the spotlight.

The humans had visited, and Josiah didn't know what to think of them, especially their leader. He had the band's future in his hands, but he hadn't told Josiah anything. He'd just looked around with his intense gaze, taking everything in.

"And you're sure no one will agree to become your beta?"

Josiah sighed. "I already asked the older band members. The ones who stayed with me long enough to listen to what I had to say laughed in my face. The others took one look at me and turned around to leave."

"I wish I could do more to help you."

"Knowing I can call you anytime to whine is enough. I don't know what I would do if I didn't have you."

"You'll never have to find out because I'm not going anywhere. You can do this, Josiah. I know you can, and so does the council. They wouldn't have asked you to become the alpha otherwise. You'll find a way around it. I know it."

Josiah hoped that Nico's faith in him wasn't misplaced. God knew Nico trusted him more than he trusted himself.

Luther sat at the head of the table and looked down its length. It was strange to see an empty seat, but he was also relieved it was empty. He'd never liked Randy, and now, he knew why.

Luther wished there was more he could do to Randy. He wanted to punish him for going against his orders, but unfortunately for him, Randy had been following other orders, coming from people higher up than Luther in the hierarchy. That was why the only thing Luther had been able to do was to kick his ass out of the team, and he knew he was going to pay for it sooner rather than later. In the meantime, both his mission and the forest were safe.

"Who do we still have on our list?" he asked.

He knew the answer to that, but it wouldn't be a bad thing

to go over the territories they'd already visited and the ones still missing.

"The deer, the bats, and the raccoons," Dean said.

Luther nodded. "Any of those who might cause trouble?"

"Not as far as I know. I'm not the right person to ask, though."

But Chris and Jacob weren't here, and they weren't part of the team. No matter how much Luther trusted them, they were still shifters, which meant they were part of the people he and his team were investigating. "Possibly the raccoons," Suzanne said.

"What have you heard?"

"Nothing much, just a whisper here and there."

"That's not a lot to work with."

"What about the coyotes?" Miriam asked. "Aren't we supposed to visit that territory again?"

Luther leaned back in his chair. They were supposed to visit the band again, but he wasn't looking forward to it.

The coyotes were the problem child in this situation. Their alpha was young, and from what Luther had seen, the band didn't respect him. So far, it hadn't been a problem, but he doubted it would last long. He should have written that in his reports, but instead, he'd kept it secret.

He knew why.

For some reason, Luther was fascinated by Josiah. More importantly, he liked him, and he hoped Josiah would be able to keep the coyotes under control. He'd just become the alpha, and Luther wanted to give him time to settle into the role and earn the coyotes' respect.

This was a problem waiting to happen, though. From what Luther had heard around the forest, the coyotes were hard to deal with. It all stemmed from the way Josiah's father and brother had led the band, and they hadn't left Josiah easy shoes to fill. They'd both been abusive assholes, and it was obvious the band was used to deal with that kind of alpha. They probably didn't know what to do with Josiah, and the fact that he was a carrier didn't help matters.

Luther tapped his fingertips onto the table. He needed to write up another report. His superior was becoming impatient, and he wanted Luther to get to the point and make a decision. It wasn't an easy one to make, though, especially not since Luther didn't want the forest and the shifters who lived here to have to change the way they lived. As far as it looked, even though there had been a fight a little while ago, they had everything under control.

"We'll visit them again," he agreed. "Once we're done with the others." That would give Josiah time to try to get the coyotes under control. Luther didn't even care if it was only a façade. As long as everyone was respectful and appeared to follow Josiah's orders when he and his team visited the band, he would be happy to put that in his report and go his way.

"I can't wait to go home," Miriam said.

She had a baby girl at home, so Josiah wasn't surprised.

"I'm more than happy here," Marlow answered. He'd been quiet until now, but then, he always was.

"That's because you like living in the forest. I'm sure the shifters can't wait for us to leave, though."

That was probably the truth. No one liked having people sticking their noses in their business, but especially not when those people were humans who were supposed to decide your fate. Luther wasn't looking forward to going home like Miriam was, but then, he didn't have anyone waiting for him there. His apartment was empty. He didn't have a family or a significant other. He had his parents and his sister, of course, but they had their own lives. Luther didn't see them anywhere as often as he wanted, but it made sense.

"I don't know," Marlow said. "I think that a lot of them are curious about us and wouldn't mind if we stayed."

That was news to Luther. He wasn't blind, and he'd seen the distrust and sometimes hatred aimed at them. "Wouldn't they?" he asked.

Marlow shrugged. "You might not realize that since you're

our team leader, but I know it for sure. I've been talking to a lot of people."

"On your own?"

"I promise I was careful and that I didn't put myself in more danger than I could deal with. These shifters are just people, though. They want the same things we do."

"Except you can't turn into a badger," Suzanne pointed out.

"So? It doesn't make me more human than they are. They're good people, just like we are."

"The coyotes wouldn't be in this situation if their alpha had been a good person."

Marlow waved Suzanne's words away. "There are bad humans, too. It's the same everywhere. It doesn't mean that the entire forest wants to kill us. I wish you could see that."

Luther wished the same. He hadn't known what to expect when he'd accepted this job, but now, he was glad he had. Just like a lot of humans, he'd always wondered what happened in the forests. That was where shifters had been relegated after the war and where they had been locked up since then. What he'd found was very different than what most people thought happened here, and he still didn't know how to deal with it. These people weren't just animals like a lot of people thought. Like Marlow had said, they were humans, and he deserved to be treated as such.

The way they were locked up in forests didn't sit right with Luther, but he was only one man. How was he supposed to change that on his own?

"Maybe you should stick around," Suzanne said.

"I would if I could. I like these people more than I like my own family, so it wouldn't be a problem."

Luther cleared his throat to get everyone's attention again. As much as he enjoyed listening to his team talking, they had work to do. "Who do you think we should start with?"

Suzanne turned her attention back to her phone. "I don't think it makes a difference. Since I heard people talking, though, maybe the raccoons? The deer and bats should be easy enough, and once that's done, we can go back to coyotes."

"What about the skunks?" Dean asked.

"What about them?"

"They weren't happy to see us when we went."

"Not being happy to see us doesn't mean we have to visit them again. I didn't see anything that gave me doubts when we did. Did you?"

Dean shook his head. "Not see, but I talked with the future alpha. His father isn't happy about our presence in the forest, and while he played nice while we were there, it might not last."

Luther was surprised to find out that Dean had talked to a shifter on his own, too. What was happening to his team? "Who did you say you talk to?"

To Luther's surprise, Dean's cheeks turned pink and he looked away. "The future alpha. His name is Jasper. He's Alpha Rhodes' son."

Luther remembered him. He hadn't been happy to find out what the skunks had done to their carriers, but he didn't have any authority on them, and his superior wouldn't care because carriers were shifters. "Did he mention his father was planning something?"

"No, but he's worried."

Luther nodded. "We'll add the surfeit to our list, then. We can visit them after the coyotes." Maybe in the meantime, Luther would find out what Dean knew about Jasper and his father.

ABOUT THE AUTHOR

Catherine is the creator of several series, most of them para-normal, including the Whitedell Pride Series and the Gillham Pack Series. While she graduated in translation, she decided to go the writer's way because it was more fun to create her own stories and characters.

She's been living in Italy for more than twenty years, but she's a daughter of the North—Belgium to be precise—and she misses it so much that she's already planning to move back.

She loves pizza—probably too much—her son, her pets, and of course, books. She sneaks some reading time into her schedule every time she has five minutes free from writing, demands from her various pets and son, and lastly, house-work.

Connect with her:

lievens.catherine@gmail.com
BookBub: https://www.bookbub.com/authors/catherine-lievens
Website: https://authorcatherinelievens.com/
Facebook: https://www.facebook.com/catherine.lievens.9
Facebook Group: https://www.facebook.com/groups/411788002341528/
Twitter: https://twitter.com/authorCLievens
Newsletter: https://authorcatherinelievens.com/newsletter/